A MOST UNUSUAL CHRISTMAS

Cressida Hadley is delighted when Lord Bromley and his family are unexpectedly obliged to spend Christmas at her family home, the Abbey. True, Bromley's brother has a broken leg, her father and the earl have taken an instant dislike to each other, and the Dowager Lady Bromley drinks too much — but Cressida is convinced she can overcome these difficulties to arrange a merry holiday season. However, she has not taken into consideration the possibility that she might fall in love with Lord Bromley himself . . .

FENELLA J. MILLER

A MOST UNUSUAL CHRISTMAS

Complete and Unabridged

LINFORD
Leicester

First published in Great Britain in 2017

First Linford Edition
published 2017

A catalogue record for this book is available
from the British Library.

ISBN 978–1–4448–3438–3

Published by
F. A. Thorpe (Publishing)
Anstey, Leicestershire

Set by Words & Graphics Ltd.
Anstey, Leicestershire
Printed and bound in Great Britain by
T. J. International Ltd., Padstow, Cornwall

This book is printed on acid-free paper

1

December 1815

'Mama, Amanda, you must be freezing. It's damnably cold in here.' Guy gathered up the fur from his knees and carefully tucked it around his sister and his mother.

'It's been snowing for the past hour, Bromley. Should we not have stopped at the last inn and taken shelter from the blizzard?' Harry, his junior by eight years and heir to his earldom and vast estates, shifted his weight and the carriage rocked.

'Sit still, Harry, or you'll have us in the ditch,' Amanda snapped. 'Mama, I'm going to cast up my accounts if I do not get out of this carriage immediately.' His sister was an indifferent traveller and had been begging him to curtail their journey for this past hour.

He sincerely regretted agreeing to spend the Christmas period with his uncle in Suffolk when the weather was so inclement. It would have been better to remain at home in Hertfordshire, but his siblings and mama had been determined to celebrate Christ's name day with their cousins where there would be parties and jollity. For his maternal uncle, Christmas was enjoyed in the old-fashioned way. Since his wife had died from the wasting sickness two years ago, there had been nothing to celebrate at Bromley Court.

Guy leaned over and was about to unhook the leather strap that held the window when his world turned upside down. As the carriage tumbled side-ways, he braced himself against the sides and prayed his family would suffer no serious harm from the accident. His sister's scream ripped the air, and then he was crushed beneath a tangle of arms and legs as the vehicle settled with an ominous crack on its side.

'Everyone, remain still!' he exclaimed.

'Don't try to get up until I can discover exactly what has occurred.'

'Bromley, you nincompoop, we've overturned! Even I know that.' Harry's voice came from the other side of the carriage.

'Mama, Amanda, are you hurt?' Guy carefully removed his right hand from the side of the carriage and gently touched the inert form resting on his chest. This meant taking the weight entirely on his left arm. He was fairly sure it was his sister who was crushed against him, and she was disturbingly still.

'I am unhurt, Bromley. I landed on top of your brother and he broke my fall. Why isn't Amanda speaking to us?'

'She's unconscious, Mama, but from my investigation I think her merely stunned.' He had no idea if this was the case, but thought it wise not to send his mother into a conniption fit.

The clattering and noise that had been coming from the horses stopped, and Fred, his head coachman, banged on the side of the coach. 'My lord, you must keep still. The carriage is perilously balanced above a deep ditch. The axle broke and this tipped us over.'

'Understood. Use the horses to pull the carriage upright, but be quick — Lady Amanda is injured.'

'There's a drive leading to a big house — I've sent Tom on one of the horses to fetch help. We'll have you all out of there right smart, my lord.'

'Excellent. Are the horses unharmed?'

'Yes, my lord, but I fear the carriage is done for.'

Amanda groaned and tried to move. 'Hush, little one,' Guy told her. 'You must remain still. We shall be out of here soon and in the warm.'

As he spoke, he was aware that icy water was already seeping through the door, and his heavy travelling coat was becoming unpleasantly wet. He daren't move, as this might tip the carriage further into the ditch.

'Harry, I shall need you and Mama to move backwards very slowly in a minute. Be ready to stop if we start to slide further into the ditch.'

His back was already wet, and if he didn't get himself clear of the water he feared his sister would soon be damp as well as concussed.

'Fred, tie the harness to the wheels and get the remaining animals to take the strain. We cannot wait for help to arrive. We must do something now.'

His coachman shouted his agreement. A few minutes later the coach rocked and then slowly moved towards the road. 'Right, my lord, all secure. You won't tip no further.'

'Harry, Mama, roll towards the road. Do it now.' Guy placed one arm around his sister and then threw his considerable weight forward. The carriage groaned and creaked as if alive, and slowly righted itself. They were now jammed into the well of the carriage, and his sister was still not fully conscious. He had managed to protect her as the vehicle rolled and was sure she had suffered no further harm.

The door opened, and Fred pulled down the steps and assisted Guy's mother to her feet. His brother had remained where he was. 'I didn't want to say anything, Bromley, but I'm damned if I haven't broken my leg,' Harry said.

'Stay where you are, old fellow. I'll hand Amanda out and then we can see to you.'

A tall young man stepped forward through the blizzard and held out his arms to receive Amanda's semiconscious body. 'Allow me, sir. I'm Richard Hadley, and I live at the Abbey. I can hold her until help arrives.'

Guy handed his sister across. 'Here, Hadley — wrap her in this fur. There are several others in here. Would you be kind enough to give them to my mother?'

Once he was sure his family were as warm and safe as they could be in the circumstances, Guy turned his attention to his brother. Judging from the angle of his leg, it was a nasty break, and moving him without doing further damage was going to be all but impossible. The snow was muffling all sound, and he doubted if he'd hear rescue approaching until it arrived. He strained his ears and was certain there was a horse approaching at a gallop. Tom reined in and told them a carriage was on its way.

'Return to the house, Tom. Tell them my brother has broken his leg and will require a trestle to get him to safety.'

The boy touched his cap and disappeared into the swirling whiteness.

* * *

Cressida was gazing out of the window at the flurries of snow. 'I think this year we'll have a white Christmas, Papa. It's already settling.'

Her father, Colonel John Hadley, peered at her over his newspaper. 'I shall have to cancel our New Year ball if that's the case.'

Sarah, her younger sister by three

years, jumped to her feet and ran to the window. 'It might be pretty, but I hate the snow. I shan't be able to ride, and we shall have no visitors at all until it goes.'

'Where is your brother?' the colonel asked. 'I've not seen him since last night.'

Cressida and Sarah exchanged a worried glance. 'I believe he stayed in the village, Papa,' said the former. 'Some of his friends from Oxford were passing through.'

'As long as it's not those rackety fellows from London. They will lead Richard into further mischief, and I might not be able to extricate him next time.'

Cressida was about to turn away when Sarah clutched her arm. 'Look, there's a youth in livery galloping down the drive. If I'm not mistaken, he's riding a carriage horse.'

Immediately their father was on his feet. 'There must have been an accident. Girls, inform the housekeeper that we need chambers preparing.' He strode from the room to organise a rescue.

Cressida hurried after him, eager to hear how many visitors they might expect. 'I sincerely hope no one has been seriously hurt,' she said. 'The weather is worsening, and I doubt anyone will get through to the doctor in the next village.'

'Mama taught you everything she knew about healing and herbs.' Her father smiled down at her. 'I doubt there's another young lady in the county who could set a bone or stitch a wound the way you can.'

'Sarah, please find Miller whilst I prepare my basket and arrange for hot water to be fetched.' Cressida paused as something occurred to her. 'I think it might be wise to have the downstairs apartment made ready in case anyone is seriously injured. It will be far easier to nurse them down here. Don't forget, there will be servants as well as the travellers to provide for.'

Her sister ran off. There was no need to remind her about warning their head groom — Sarah preferred animals to humans, and her first concern would be for the horses. Since their beloved mama had died three years ago, it had fallen to Cressida to take over the running of the household, and all thought of having a Season had been put to one side.

For Cressida this had been a relief more than anything else, for she had been dreading spending several months being ogled and crushed at a variety of routs and balls. The colonel wished Sarah to make her come-out in March next year — at eighteen years of age, she would be a year or two older than most debutantes — but her sister was equally reluctant to go to London and be paraded like a prize heifer in front of suitable bachelors.

As she passed through the impressive entrance hall, Grimshaw, the butler, opened the front door and an icy blast of snow and wind filled the space. She waited in order to hear exactly what had transpired at the end of the drive. Knowing the extent of any injuries that had been sustained would make her task much easier.

The young coachman refused to come in after delivering his message, but vaulted onto his waiting horse and thundered off down the drive again. The colonel appeared in his riding coat and beaver on the gallery and came down the steps three at a time. 'Earl Bromley, Lady Bromley, his mother, and his brother and sister were in the coach that overturned,' he explained. 'Lady Amanda appears to be the only one injured, which is a relief. I shall leave Miller to arrange suitable accommodation for our unexpected guests. I'm sending a carriage to collect them, my dear, and I'll accompany it. It's damned dark outside and barely two o'clock. Get Cook to bring dinner forward — no doubt they'll be sharp-set after this mishap and want to eat as soon as possible.'

'They will be without their luggage and will require fresh garments,' Cressida said. 'However, I'll have to wait until I meet this family of aristocrats before finding them something suitable.'

'I expect they'll need personal servants too. Get Grimshaw to find somebody for the earl and his brother, and Miller can do the same for the ladies.'

He strode off to the side door that led directly to the stables, leaving his daughter to hurry to her still room at the rear of the house. It was here that she prepared the concoctions and tisanes she prescribed for both indoor and outdoor staff. Possibly she would have been burned as a witch two hundred years ago, but nowadays most people were more enlightened. The local physician was in his dotage and still believed that everything could be cured by bleeding. For this reason, her mother had taken over the task of doctoring on their estate and had passed on her extensive knowledge to Cressida.

By the time she had assembled the things she thought she might need, a quarter of an hour had passed. She carried a basket to the downstairs apartment that had been occupied by her grandfather. Whilst her father had been fighting the French, her mother and her siblings had remained with Grandfather. When the war ended last year, the colonel had finally come home to take over the estate, which had been run in his absence by a highly competent estate manager. Cressida's eyes filled as she recalled the dreadful winter three years ago when Mama had died from the putrid sore throat. Her father had not heard of her demise until they were out of mourning, and by then there was little point in him returning.

Her brother Richard had been sent down from Oxford shortly after Mama died, and since then had fallen from one scrape into another. His intention had been to join the colonel's regiment, but new officers were not needed now that Bonaparte was safely captured. Where was he? Why hadn't he returned last night?

Cressida pushed her concerns aside; he was a grown man and capable of taking care of himself. She must concentrate on helping the occupants from the coach. Although the Abbey had been in the Hadley family for generations, they were not part of the elite that ruled the country. They had no wish to be ennobled, and kept well away from politics. The thought of having such toplofty folk staying with them over the Christmas period filled Cressida with foreboding.

The house was bustling with maids and footmen fetching and carrying items for the underused apartment downstairs. This had been under holland covers since Cressida's grandfather had died, and she hoped the rooms would not be damp. Miller was directing operations and Cressida was pleased to see that fires had been lit and the chambers were no longer freezing.

'The beds are made and warming pans have been passed through,' Miller announced. 'I've cleared the table by the washstand for you, Miss Hadley; will that be sufficient for your needs?'

'Thank you, Miller,' Cressida answered. 'You've thought of everything. I expect Lord Bromley and his family will be here shortly. As soon as we can see their size and shape, we can find them fresh clothes.'

'I've already found nightshirts and nightgowns, underpinnings and wraps — I can have everything else collected as soon as they arrive. I've put Earl Bromley in the best apartment, with the Dowager Lady Bromley next door to him, and everything is also ready in the smaller guest chamber. Until we know who is going to be sleeping down here, I cannot complete my preparations.'

Cressida put down her basket as the housekeeper was speaking and began to arrange the things she thought she might need. 'There must be at least two coachmen, and they will need accom-modation outside with our grooms and gardeners.'

'Miss Sarah has seen to that. It's a good thing the pantries are well-stocked because of the Christmas festivities. I doubt anyone will be able to deliver extra provisions until the snow has gone.'

Once she was sure everything was as prepared as it could be, Cressida ran upstairs and put on her stout boots, muffler and cape just in case she was required to go outside and assist when the carriage returned. She was on her way downstairs when there was a second hammering on the door.

Grimshaw spoke briefly to the person on the doorstep and then turned to her. 'Lord Bromley's brother has broken his leg. They want a trestle to carry him back here.'

'Send word outside. I must go too. Have my horse saddled whilst I collect what I need.'

The awaited carriage emerged from the snow. Young Hadley climbed in with Amanda and his mother followed suit. As the coachman was turning the vehicle, a horseman arrived at a canter, and a large gentleman in a many-caped riding coat dismounted.

'Colonel Hadley at your service,' he said. 'Your groom thundered past us a moment ago. Am I to assume that someone else is injured apart from the young lady?'

'My brother has broken his leg,' said Guy. 'I've taken the liberty of sending my under-coachman to fetch men and a trestle in order to transport him to your house.'

'Excellent. It could be a while before they arrive, so you might as well wait inside your carriage. Your coachmen and I might as well take your horses to shelter — there's damn all we can do here.' Colonel Hadley collected the reins of one of the carriage horses and

Tom scrambled onto the back of another and led the third. 'Where the devil's my son's nag?'

'Mr Hadley arrived on foot, sir,' Tom told him.

The colonel muttered something unrepeatable under his breath and then he and Tom vanished into the swirling whiteness. The snow was falling more heavily now, and a biting easterly wind flapped Guy's coat about his legs. Waiting inside the carriage was a sensible notion; at least he'd be out of the way of this damn wind.

When he walked around to the far side of the vehicle he discovered that the wheels were precariously balanced on the edge of the ditch. If he attempted to climb in that way, he might well overturn the vehicle again. He had no option but to remain outside and hope that the men with the trestle arrived promptly.

'How are you doing, Harry? Here, let me put that fur over your legs, and then I'll close the door — there's no point in both of us perishing from the cold.'

His brother managed a weak chuckle. 'They'll think you're a snowman when they arrive. My leg hurts like the very devil and I can't feel my toes.'

'There's nothing I can do about it, but help is on its way. It must be half a mile to the house and it will take the stretcher-bearers a quarter of an hour at least to reach us. If you don't mind, I'm going to stand out of the wind until they arrive.'

Guy propped himself against the front of the coach, glad to be a little warmer. Then there was the sound of voices, and if he was not mistaken someone on horseback was accompanying them. Four men carrying a trestle panted up beside the carriage. They were well wrapped up against the cold, and he was delighted to see that several blankets had been fetched along as well. The horseman dismounted and approached him.

'Lord Bromley, I am Cressida Hadley. I've come to take care of your brother.'

2

Cressida ignored the look of stupefaction on Bromley's face and stepped past him to the carriage, 'I take it he's in here?'

'Thank you for your offer, Miss Hadley, but we have no need of your assistance.' The large snow-encrusted shape bowed and beckoned to the men with the trestle. 'Bring that here. I need to remove the blankets.'

Cressida ignored him and wrenched open the carriage door, knowing that her medical bag and splints would be handed to her by one of the men. 'Good afternoon, sir. I am Miss Hadley, and I've come to splint your leg so that you can be moved to the Abbey.'

The young man, who was slumped against the squabs, managed a weak smile and raised a hand in salute but was in too much distress to answer. His features were pinched and his lips blue with cold. Cressida prayed they were not too late to prevent a tragedy. She dropped to her knees in the snow and gently examined his leg. It was a nasty break, but a clean one, and there was no bone protruding through his skin. Without turning, she called out, 'Please hand me the splints and bandages from the trestle.'

'Here you are, Miss Hadley, and I beg your pardon for my less-than-civil greeting.' Lord Bromley passed her the items she wanted.

Quickly she removed the small bottle of opiate and a flask of brandy. 'My lord, you must drink this. It will make the next few minutes far easier for you.' She carefully tipped a generous measure into the silver cup that accompanied the flask and added sufficient laudanum to knock the patient out.

In order to reach him, she would have to climb into the vehicle. Her arms were not long enough and the injured man was too weak to stretch forward.

'Let me do it; it will be easier for both of you.' Lord Bromley removed the cup from her hand and she moved aside. His arms stretched easily and he tipped the liquid into his brother's mouth. 'We'll soon have you warm and comfortable, old fellow. Just sleep now.'

Fortunately the blizzard had temporarily abated, and Cressida could now see to work. She watched the patient's eyes flicker closed. She removed a sharp blade from her bag and deftly slit the boot on the broken leg. 'Bill, get round to the back of the coach with your men, and lean all your weight on it.' The earl would have to climb into the carriage and then support his brother whilst she straightened the injured limb and applied the splints to either side.

Without her having to explain what she required, the gentleman in question removed his coat and dropped it into the snow. Then as soon as he heard the men take the strain, he scrambled across the squabs and positioned himself behind his brother. 'Do what you have to, Miss Hadley, and do it quickly. I don't like my brother's colour one bit.'

Cressida had performed this procedure twice before and was confident she could do it successfully this time. She gripped the unconscious man's ankle and pulled steadily. For a moment nothing happened, and then she felt the bones grind into place. The splints were lying ready and she was able to maintain the pressure whilst she slipped the lengths of wood on either side of the break. A few minutes later Lord Harry was ready to be lifted from the carriage. 'I'm done, my lord,' Cressida said. 'We can move him now.'

In the gloom of the carriage interior she saw him shake his head. 'He will be too heavy for you, Miss Hadley. We must wait until one of your men comes round.'

'Nonsense, I am perfectly capable of bearing his weight. Right — I'm going to lift his legs and walk backwards, and you must move him towards the carriage door. Once we have him halfway out, it will be safe for two of my men to come round and complete the manoeuvre.'

Guy didn't argue, and together they proceeded to edge the patient forwards. As soon as the legs were outside and his derriere was on the step, Guy shouted for assistance, and immediately two of the stretcher-bearers arrived at Cressida's side.

'I'll fetch the trestle and arrange the blankets so you can put your brother in the centre,' she said. 'They're not just for warmth, but also to keep him still whilst he's carried down the drive.'

Soon the patient was snugly wrapped, and four men picked up the corners of the trestle and began the slow trudge down the snow-covered drive. It hardly seemed civil for Cressida to ride back when the earl had no mount. The horse that had been sent round for her was a sturdy animal and should be able to bear both their weights for so short a journey.

'Lord Bromley, you can ride pillion if you wish.'

'I thank you for your kind offer, but I shall walk with my brother. You go on ahead, Miss Hadley. You have done more than enough already.'

She was too cold to argue the point, so turned to scramble into the saddle unaided. But Guy was behind her in seconds and, grasping her around the waist, tossed her up. The saddle was slippery and his effort so vigorous that she was unable to grasp onto the pommel and flew straight over the gelding to land flat on her back in the snow.

How ridiculous! How humiliating! She scarcely had time to collect her thoughts before the wretched man was beside her again and had her back on her feet. Before she could protest, he was vigorously dusting off the snow.

'I do beg your pardon, Miss Hadley. That was entirely my fault.'

'Stop, sir. You've done enough harm to me already. Kindly remove yourself and join your brother. I shall be safer on my own.'

His hands dropped as if she'd suddenly become red-hot, and with a curt nod he strode off, leaving her to struggle onto the saddle unaided. Often she had bemoaned the fact she was unnaturally tall for a female, but this afternoon she was glad her leg was long enough to allow her to stretch out and push her foot into the single stirrup iron.

She clicked her tongue and the gelding moved away smoothly, eager to return to the warmth of his stable. By the time she passed the earl, she was cantering and made no effort to slow her pace. He was obliged to dive head first into the hedge in order to avoid being mowed down. His language made her ears burn and she thought that perhaps she might have been foolish to antagonise her unwanted guest.

A groom was waiting to take her

horse when she arrived, and she was relieved she didn't have to negotiate the cobbled stable yard. An ever-vigilant footman had the front door open as she reached the top step. She paused to scrape her boots before entering. There was no time for her to change her garments, although she was decidedly damp from her tumble. Her first priority was to attend to the girl who had been injured in the accident.

She tossed her cloak and gloves to the servant and ran lightly upstairs. Lady Amanda would not have been placed downstairs; that apartment would be needed for Lord Harry and his broken leg.

* * *

It took Guy several minutes to extricate himself from the hedge, and the trestle with his brother was already out of sight. Even so, he could hear the sniggering coming from the men who carried him, and his fury returned. He would have words to say to that young lady when he saw her next. He was Earl Bromley — a man of dignity and substance — and nobody had ever had the temerity to tip him onto his backside until today. Then he realised how pompous he was being, for hadn't he just done the same to her?

He lengthened his stride and soon caught up with his brother, and was pleased to see Harry greet him with a grin. 'I think you could call it a draw, Bromley. I can't wait to see who scores the next point.'

'Miss Hadley is going to regret tipping me into a hedge, brother, but I intend to bide my time. Revenge is a dish best eaten cold.' Guy laughed and squeezed his brother's shoulder. For the first time in two years he actually had something to look forward to.

When he offered to take a turn with the trestle, the men refused, saying they were happy to continue. Eventually the shape of a substantial house emerged through the whiteness, and he was impressed by what he saw. He fully expected to be directed to a side door; even outdoor men carrying a member of the family would not be allowed to go in through the front door at Bromley Court. However, they headed straight for the steps, and he quickly positioned himself at the rear of the makeshift stretcher to ensure that his brother didn't slide off when it was tilted. 'We have arrived, Harry,' he said. 'We will soon have you comfortably settled.'

From his blanket cocoon, his brother replied quite cheerfully, 'Whatever it was that Miss Hadley gave me to drink has worked wonderfully well. My leg no longer hurts; and if I'm cold, I certainly don't feel it.'

As they reached the door, four uniformed flunkies emerged and took over the task of carrying Harry. The outdoor men vanished into the once-more swirling snow, and Guy followed the trestle inside. He was greeted by his mother, who looked remarkably well for someone with two children injured so recently in a carriage accident.

'You are here at last, Bromley. Miss Hadley is waiting to take care of Harry. I shall take you to the chamber he is to occupy.'

'How is Amanda? Does she have a concussion?'

His mother shook her head vigorously. 'Indeed not, my dear boy. She was merely stunned and is now fully recovered. Miss Hadley has suggested she remain in bed today but can get up as usual tomorrow.'

'That is good news indeed, Mama. I'll go and see her as soon as Harry is comfortable.'

'Come along, Bromley; the apartment is this way. The Abbey is built on the remains of an ancient building, but has been refurbished and is remarkably comfortable. I do declare it to be almost as large as Bromley Court, and it's certainly far warmer.'

Guy looked around with interest and saw nothing to detract from his mother's enthusiasm. The passageways were stone, but the centre of the floor was carpeted and the walls were freshly painted. A variety of interesting portraits and landscapes hung at regular intervals.

'Miss Hadley has everything arranged for us, and you will be pleased with your accommodation, for it's as fine as any I have seen.'

Guy gritted his teeth — he was becoming irritated by his mother's constant references to Miss Hadley. It would appear that this young lady had far too much to say for herself and was given too much sway in this household. 'Is there a Mrs Hadley?' he asked.

His mother halted so suddenly that he cannoned into her, and only by good fortune did they both not end up on the floor. 'Tarnation take it, Mama, you almost had us over.'

'Kindly moderate your language, Bromley. I don't wish to hear such things, especially when we are uninvited guests at this place.'

'I beg your pardon, Mama, but it's

been a trying day. Now, you've yet to answer my question.' They resumed their dash down the corridor and she replied as she hurried.

'The colonel's wife died three years ago, and Miss Hadley has been running the household since then.' She stopped in front of an open door and gestured towards the interior of the chamber. 'This is where Harry has been taken. I shan't come in as I should just be in the way.' She almost ran back down the passageway. This was strange indeed, thought Guy, as she was infamous for her indolence.

Again the appointments were elegant and the room delightfully warm. This was the sitting room. Voices were coming from an open door at the far end, and Guy strode towards it. He was about to announce himself when he hesitated in the doorway, not wishing to distract Miss Hadley from her task. There was no necessity for him to offer his assistance, as her brother was already at her side. The two of them were deftly stripping Harry, and a waiting servant — presumably a valet, as he was not in uniform — slid a nightshirt over him, ensuring that at no time was there an unnecessary exposure of skin.

'Don't dither in the doorway, my lord. Either come in or go out.' Miss Hadley's words reminded him what an irritating young lady she was.

'I see that Lord Harry is in capable hands, so I shall remove myself.'

Harry raised an eyebrow, and Guy had an unaccountable desire to throw something at him. He retreated and couldn't prevent himself from smiling despite his annoyance. This was a most unusual household, and spending the next two weeks here was going to be interesting.

His sense of direction was excellent and he had no difficulty finding his way to the main part of the house. Double doors stood open to the right of the front door, and he strode across the vast expanse of chequered floor and walked into the grand drawing room.

His mother was sitting opposite Colonel Hadley and appeared to be engrossed in what he was saying. Even when his father had been alive, Guy could not remember seeing her so animated. He remained unnoticed in the shadows and watched them. It was as if a veil had been lifted from his eyes and for the first time he saw his parent as an attractive woman, not just as his mother.

God's teeth! The last thing he needed was for her to become enamoured of this gentleman. She was the Dowager Countess Bromley; and the colonel, although obviously wealthy, was not a member of the *ton*. Guy stepped forward, intending to interrupt their *tête-à-tête*, when somebody collided with him. Taken by surprise, he was unable to keep his balance and pitched forward flat on his face.

'Good grief, Bromley, whatever are you playing at? Do not remain down there — you are getting in the way of

Miss Sarah,' his mother said unsympathetically.

A second female voice spoke from above him: 'I do beg your pardon, my lord. I had no idea you were lurking in the corner and about to step in front of me.'

Guy was tempted to remain where he was. His dignity had been severely dented for the second time that day and he was not enjoying the experience at all. Before he stood up, he needed to control his fury, as what he wanted to say to the young lady who had knocked him over would not endear him to the colonel, who had so kindly taken them in.

Then Hadley was kneeling beside him. 'Dammit, are you hurt? Stay where you are — I'll send for my daughter.'

The colonel's words prompted him to surge to his feet. 'I am perfectly well, thank you, sir. I was just remaining still until I was certain I would not be bowled over again.'

Miss Sarah was laughing openly, and this did nothing to restore his temper. 'I apologise again, my lord. Won't you come in and join us? I give you my solemn oath it will be quite safe to walk across and join Lady Bromley.'

He was about to respond with a pithy reply but the words remained unsaid. The young lady standing beside him was a diamond of the first water. Her hair was the colour of ripe corn, her eyes periwinkle-blue, and he believed he had never seen such a vision of loveliness.

'Miss Sarah, it is I who should apologise for stepping in your way. I'm delighted to accept your invitation.' He offered his arm as if they were at a formal occasion, and with a sweet smile she placed her hand on it. The girl's head came to his shoulder — a perfect height for a young lady.

He led her down the length of the drawing room and then bowed her into a chair. He took an identical seat beside her and decided that despite Harry's broken leg, and the ruination of his new travelling carriage, he was rather glad the accident had taken place. Without fate's intervention, they would have driven past the Abbey and would never have known this delightful young lady existed.

His reverie was rudely interrupted by his mother. 'Bromley, you are wool-gathering. Colonel Hadley has invited us to stay until after the New Year. As I doubt that poor Harry will be able to travel for several weeks, I have accepted his kind invitation. I hope you have no objection.'

He raised his head and met her quizzical glance. 'None at all, Mama. As we have no carriage, we could not continue our journey unless we hired a vehicle.' He turned his attention to his host. 'Thank you, sir. We are most obliged to you. As soon as the weather improves, I shall send one of my coachmen to find our luggage and personal servants.'

Only as he finished his sentence did

he remember that he was still in disarray. He glanced down in horror at his mud-spattered breeches and revolting boots. How could he have appeared in the drawing room without improving his appearance? What was the matter with him?

3

Cressida tied the last bandage in place and stepped away from the bed. 'There, Lord Harry — your leg is set, and I'm sure it will heal without leaving you with a limp. However, you must remain in bed for a while, and then only go as far as your sitting room.'

'Thank you, Miss Hadley; I'm most obliged for your assistance. Perhaps you could get one of your men to knock me out a pair of crutches, and then I can hop about once you give me permission to get up.'

'I'll do that straightaway. At least there will be no problem finding you something appropriate to wear, as you must remain in your nightshirt for the next few days.'

'I doubt you'll find anything to fit my brother. He's a prodigious size — must be a throwback, because no other

Bromley's as broad or as tall.' He grinned and she couldn't help but respond. He was really a very charming young man. 'Come to think of it, he's the only one with dark hair and dark eyes in the family. My long-departed father had light brown hair, and no doubt you have already observed that my mama and sister have the same colouring as myself.'

'Lady Amanda has hair the colour of autumn leaves and the most beautiful green eyes — she's the image of Lady Bromley.'

The under-footman who had been promoted to serve as Harry's valet had put the hastily constructed wooden frame across his lordship's legs and then carefully pulled over the covers. He was now hovering anxiously, waiting for further instructions.

'You need to rest, my lord, so I'll leave you in the capable hands of Bernard,' Cressida said. 'You also have a chambermaid at your service, and between them they'll supply everything you require. I'll call in to see you after dinner.' She nodded at the valet. 'Fetch me immediately if Lord Harry develops a fever or his condition deteriorates in any way.'

The skirts of her riding habit clung unpleasantly to her ankles; it was high time she changed her clothes. The Hadley family were not known for their sartorial elegance: they dressed for practicality, not fashion. However, she and Sarah had been obliged recently to replenish their wardrobes, and now had a splendid collection of the new high-waisted gowns that were fashion-able.

However, before she went to her chambers she must speak to Richard. He was in his bed, looking decidedly sorry for himself. ' Where were you last night, and what has happened to your horse?' she asked him.

'I was gambling and lost him in a wager. There's no need to look daggers, Cressie. I'm miserable enough already. God knows what the colonel will say when he finds out I'm up to my ears in debt. It's not just a case of remaining here on a repairing lease — I owe hundreds of guineas to some very unsavoury characters.'

She had suspected something of the kind, but not the appalling amount involved. 'How could you? Papa will send you to the colonies this time — he said as much when he bailed you out last year.'

Her brother shrugged as if indifferent to the thought of being banished to America. 'That's not the worst of it. I managed to escape through a window and make my way home. Those men will soon discover my whereabouts and come here to demand satisfaction.'

'Then let's pray the snow remains until after our visitors depart.' Cressida stepped over to him and felt his forehead. 'You have a slight fever; no doubt you will go down with a nasty head cold. I'll tell our parent and guests that you are indisposed and won't be joining us for dinner.'

'Before you go, tell me — how is Lady Amanda?'

'She will be fully recovered by tomorrow. Now, did you send for a tray?'

'I did, thank you. I require nothing else today but some sleep. I've been awake for thirty-six hours and trudged five miles through the snow.'

'Then I'll leave you. I've yet to change into something dry myself, and I've no wish to go down with a fever myself.'

Her abigail was waiting and had hot water and fresh undergarments ready. 'As we have guests staying, miss, are you going to put on one of your new evening gowns?'

'Good heavens, no, of course not. We stand on no ceremony here, and as these are uninvited guests they must take us as we are. Anyway, they have nothing to change into, so it would be impolite to go downstairs dressed in my new finery when they are still in their travelling clothes.'

'Mrs Miller has sent a selection of Mrs Hadley's gowns to Lady Bromley, and Miss Sarah has done the same for Lady Amanda.'

'Dinner is going to be served within half an hour, so I doubt anyone is going to change. I'm sure they will expect us to do so once their luggage arrives — but that could be several days if the snow doesn't melt.' She glanced with disinterest at the selection Jenny had put out for her. She pointed to a gown with high neck and long sleeves that would be ideal, as she wouldn't need to take a shawl.

Jenny rearranged her hair and then Cressida was ready. Although she had an expensive full-length glass, she didn't bother to look in it. She looked as she always did: a tall, plain young woman. She took after her father, whereas her brother and sister were pattern copies of their mama.

The Abbey was built in the shape of the letter C. The central part of the building was occupied by the main reception rooms on the ground floor, and the family had their rooms on the first. Guests were accommodated in the east wing, and in the west were the usual offices, while the servants' quarters were in the attics. The nursery, schoolrooms and bedchambers for a governess, nanny and nursemaids took up the remaining chambers in that wing. Needless to say, these had not been in use for many years. This meant the Bromley clan was situated a goodly distance away from Cressida's own chamber, so she was unlikely to meet any of them upstairs. They also had their own staircase, so could come and go as they pleased without disturbing the family.

As she passed her sister's room, Sarah emerged dressed as if she was attending the grandest dinner party. Cressida glanced down at her own ensemble and smiled ruefully. 'I'd no idea that we were dressing for dinner tonight. I wish you'd thought to inform me. I take it the Bromley baggage cart has arrived despite the inclement weather.'

Sarah flushed and wouldn't look directly at her. 'I don't believe that it has come, Cressie, but I wish to look my best. After all, it's not often we entertain the aristocracy.'

A snort of laughter came from behind them and they turned to find their father. He too was changed, which was quite unprecedented.

'I think it's fair to say, my love, that this will be the first time the Abbey has had such illustrious visitors. This family have never been royalist; if anything, we've veered towards Puritanism rather than extravagance.'

This was the outside of enough. At least Richard would not be parading in his evening rig as he would have done if he'd been joining them. 'I decided not to change,' Cressida said. 'As our guests are unable to do so, they might well feel uncomfortable on seeing you in your splendour.'

Sarah gestured to her gown. 'You've

time to change. There's still a few minutes before dinner will be served, and I'm sure we can delay things until you come down again.'

For a moment Cressida was tempted, but then shook her head. 'No, I stand by my previous comment. At least one of us must not put them to shame. I don't understand why you both have dressed up — neither of you take much interest in your appearance in the usual way.'

Her sister mumbled something incomprehensible and hurried away, and her father cleared his throat noisily. Only then did the reason for this change of character occur to her. Papa had obviously put on evening wear because of Lady Bromley. But which of the two gentlemen had caused this *volte-face* in her sister? Surely it couldn't be the earl? He was a dozen years her senior at the very least, and not at all suitable for someone as quiet and unconventional as Sarah. No, it must be Lord Harry.

She shook her head in disgust at her silliness. Sarah had yet to meet the young man, so it could only be Lord Bromley she was dressing to impress.

'I've yet to be introduced to the countess; I take it she's a pleasant lady?' Cressida said.

'Quite delightful,' her father replied. 'I think this Christmas is going to be most enjoyable.'

This was highly unlikely in her opinion, as having a demanding family foisted on them could only lead to disaster. She shuddered at the thought of being obliged to observe her normally irascible father dancing attendance on Lady Bromley and her sister fluttering her eyelashes at the earl. All it needed was for Lady Amanda to decide that Richard was her Prince Charming and the farce would be complete.

A bubble of laughter caught her unawares as she realised that this left Lord Harry, with his broken leg, to be her beau. Perhaps this wouldn't be so bad, as it would mean she could spend more time upstairs with him than downstairs watching her family make cakes of themselves.

★   ★   ★

The temporary valet Guy had been given had made a reasonable job of repairing his appearance. His topcoat was now spotless, his breeches sponged, and his Hessians restored to their former shininess. Hadley had kindly sent him several freshly starched stocks, so he had been able to use a fresh one. As the Hadley family were aware that the luggage carriage had not arrived, they would obviously not dress for dinner. To do so would be most uncivil in the circumstances.

He stopped to speak to his brother on the way down to dinner and was pleased to see Harry was sleeping and showed no sign of fever. He took the guests' staircase, which emerged on the east side of the vaulted entrance hall. The tall-case clock ticked noisily in the corner, and he observed that he was in good time. The drawing room was already occupied.

Guy bowed politely to Miss Hadley and Miss Sarah and inclined his head to Colonel Hadley. They reciprocated in kind and his host waved him over.

'Welcome, Bromley. Help yourself to a beverage — we're drinking champagne in honour of your unexpected arrival, but there's a selection of other things as well.'

Guy was unused to serving himself. The correct way to do things was to have a footman offer a tray upon which the selection was placed and not to require a guest to play the role of servant.

'I require nothing to drink at the moment, thank you, sir.' He made his way to the central area of the room where the three of them were positioned. He was not pleased to see that Miss Sarah and Hadley were in full evening rig. Therefore he turned his attention to the older girl.

'Miss Hadley, I wish to thank you again for your efficient and expert attention to my brother,' he said. 'I called in on the way past and can inform you he is sleeping peacefully.'

'I'm sure he will make a full recovery. As long as he remains in bed for a while, his leg should heal cleanly.' When she smiled she was transformed from ordinary into something else entirely. Although not a diamond of the first water like her sibling, she was a very attractive young lady.

'My mother is infamous for her poor timekeeping and I apologise on her behalf,' he said. 'I cannot imagine what's keeping her, as she's unable to change her ensemble.'

His companion's friendly smile vanished at his *maladroit* reference to the fact that her father and sister were in evening dress. He tried to rescue the situation.

'Miss Sarah is looking charming this evening . . . ' He stopped in mid-sentence, horrified that this comment could be interpreted to mean that Miss Hadley looked anything but attractive. His neckcloth became unaccountably tighter, and an unpleasant heat travelled from his toes to the crown of his head. 'I beg your — '

'Please, my lord, don't apologise,' Cressida said graciously. 'I know you had no intention of causing offence. Shall we talk about the weather? I believe that to be an inoffensive topic.'

She was having difficulty containing her amusement and he didn't blame her. For some reason he was blundering from one *faux pas* to another this evening, and she must think him a pompous nitwit. He bowed deeply. 'Miss Hadley, do you think the snow will remain until Christmas Day?'

Her remarkable tawny eyes were brimming with laughter as she curtsied in response. 'Indeed, my lord, I am certain of it. I fear that you and your family might well be snowed in until then.'

'I have no intention of departing

without my brother, and you have already told us he cannot travel for several weeks, so we will be remaining with you until he's fit to go.'

For some reason his remark made her laugh out loud. When she had recovered her composure, she held out her hand as if in a gesture of apology. 'I don't know why I found your comment so funny, but in the circles in which I move guests wait to be invited. Being an aristocratic gentleman, I'm sure it didn't occur to you to that it might be inconvenient to have you and your staff staying at the Abbey for several weeks.'

As soon as she spoke, he understood how arrogant he'd sounded. However, pointing this out so rudely was unacceptable. His eyes narrowed and he prepared himself to deliver a scathing set-down, but she continued, blithely unaware of his anger.

'How do you know that we don't have plans to visit family elsewhere in the country? This would now be impossible, as we can hardly leave you and your family in residence on your own.'

He swallowed a lump in his throat. She was right to castigate him; he was so used to dictating events that he hadn't even considered how their unexpected arrival might well be causing embarrassment and inconvenience to the family. He was about to apologise when she spoke again.

'As it happens, sir, we have no plans to go away, and more than enough accommodation and food to provide for any number of visitors.' She nodded and moved away to speak quietly to the butler, who was obviously waiting to announce dinner but could not do so until Guy's mother appeared.

Miss Hadley was not a young lady he could like, Guy felt. She was impertinent and disrespectful, and he had every intention of telling her so as soon as he had a suitable opportunity. Where the devil was Mama? Should he go in search of her?

Then she appeared in the doorway,

all smiles and apologies, and was immediately forgiven by everyone apart from the butler — but Grimshaw's opinion was, of course, immaterial.

'Colonel Hadley, I do apologise for being tardy. Despite the lack of luggage, I wished to look my best for our first meal together.' Mama ignored Miss Hadley, who by right she should have greeted first as the hostess for the evening, and joined the colonel and his younger daughter. She accepted a brimming glass of champagne before Guy could intervene. Alcohol and his parent were a disastrous mix. He was about to call Miss Hadley over in order to warn her that his mother would become exceedingly silly very soon, but decided to refrain. It would be amusing to see how she coped when the fun started.

Miss Sarah strode towards him, her masculine gait at odds with her feminine appearance. 'Lord Bromley, I fear Papa and I shouldn't have put on evening clothes. Until my sister reminded us, we had both forgotten your luggage was still missing. I've not worn this gown before; in fact I've never worn such an item in my life. Do you like it?'

Her ingenuous remark somewhat startled him, as he was unused to being asked his opinion on feminine apparel so boldly. 'You look *ravisante*, Miss Sarah, and I'm pleased that you took the trouble to change for us.'

'Papa has also made an effort — I think he and your mother have struck up a flirtation. I've not seen him so animated in years. Has Lady Bromley been a widow for long?'

Her abrupt manner of speaking was rather disconcerting, but he rallied and managed to answer without showing his discomfiture. 'My father died ten years ago in a hunting accident.'

'Did he break his neck in a fall?'

'No, his gun misfired.' How had the conversation turned from gowns to guns? He had no wish to discuss the manner in which his father had died, and this young lady should know better than to question him.

The bad-tempered butler announced that dinner was served; and, as was usual, everyone made their own way to the open doors that led to the dining room. Guy did not offer his arm to Miss Sarah, but she seemed unaware of his deliberate omission.

Instead of being placed at suitable intervals around the enormous mahogany table, they were squashed at one end, meaning Guy would have to make polite chit-chat with whomever he was put next to. His mother took the seat beside the colonel and the Hadley girls sat together, which meant he was now sitting on his own.

For some reason, he was unaccountably annoyed that he would not now have to converse with either of the young ladies. He watched with trepidation as his parent drained a second glass of champagne. The alcohol would go to her head very soon and turn the occasion into chaos.

4

Cressida was finding it increasingly difficult to enjoy her meal, as Lord Bromley refused to join in the conversation. No doubt he thought himself so high in the instep that he wasn't obliged to be civil. Occasionally he looked at his mother, but Cressida wasn't sure if it was anxiety or annoyance she detected in his glances.

The Dowager Countess made up for her son's lack of animation. She was rattling on about a house party she'd attended. Although the anecdotes were entertaining, nobody apart from the earl knew any of the people she was referring to, so it was difficult for Papa and herself to engage in the conversation. Fortunately his infatuation with this lady meant he'd barely noticed the absence of his son. Cressida had yet to have the opportunity to tell Sarah what had happened. Richard seemed determined to ruin his life and was too self-absorbed to understand that his actions had consequences for those who loved him.

Lady Bromley was laughing gaily and waving her hands about, much to the colonel's amusement. He had sensibly removed the crystalware so that it wouldn't be sent flying.

'Bromley, why are you sitting there like a blancmange? Have you nothing to say tonight?' Lady Bromley asked.

'Madam, even if I had anything pertinent to add to the conversation, you have left me no opportunity to speak. Your constant stream of nonsense has dominated the table.'

Cressida was shocked at his rudeness, and the colonel's expression changed. His eyes blazed and he fixed Bromley with an icy stare. Sarah put her napkin over her mouth as if trying not to laugh. The only person not reacting was her ladyship.

Lady Bromley smiled sunnily at her

irascible son. 'Well, my dear boy, you know how it is when I consume alcohol of any sort. If you don't want me to misbehave, then you should ensure that I don't imbibe.' She wagged her finger at him.

Good grief, her ladyship was foxed! Cressida realised. Small wonder her son had been looking like thunder throughout the meal, as he must have known what was about to happen. She put down her cutlery and napkin and prepared to stand. 'My lady, if you are feeling unwell, would you like me to escort you to your chamber?'

'Unwell? I'm absolutely splendid, thank you, and have no wish to go anywhere. Now, shall we finish this delicious food and allow the footmen to bring in the next course?'

The waiting servants moved forward smoothly and removed the dishes that had been placed in the centre of the table — meals were served à la française at the Abbey. The tension simmered in the air, and Cressida feared her father was going to say something unforgivable; he was not renowned for his tact, and would not care one way or the other if the staff were present when there was a lively exchange of words.

'Bromley, whilst you are under my roof you will refrain from speaking to your mother in that tone. In this house we treat our ladies with respect.'

Cressida braced herself for a full-scale row, but to her astonishment the earl picked up his napkin and waved it. 'I surrender, Colonel Hadley. Mama, I apologise most humbly for being uncivil. But could I please beg you not to consume any more wine or champagne this evening?'

His mother smiled at him and then turned her smile on her companion. 'Colonel, you must not take our family spats so seriously. We're constantly at daggers drawn, but there's no malice in it, and we forget any cross words and move on immediately.'

The colonel was not to be placated so easily, although his rigid stance relaxed somewhat. 'Bromley, I'm obliged to accept your apology, as not to do so would be churlish. However, you will refrain from speaking to anyone residing under my roof as though they're of no account. Is that understood?'

For a moment the issue hung in the balance. Cressida watched the earl closely and saw his jaw was clenched and his eyes were icy. Then he nodded, and his lips curved in a smile that fooled no one. 'I stand corrected, sir, and give you my word as a gentleman that I will curb my tongue in future.' If he had stopped there, the matter would have ended and the evening continued in a lighter vein. 'However, if I'm provoked, then I shall respond in kind. I am Earl Bromley, and do not tolerate impertinence or bad behaviour from anyone.'

The colonel surged to his feet, sending glasses and crockery in all directions. 'This is my house and you are my guest. I suggest that you find accommodation elsewhere. You are no longer welcome here.'

Bromley was also standing, and despite the acrimony between them, Cressida could not help observing they both were formidable gentlemen and both used to getting their own way. Time for the ladies to intervene before the earl was pitched out head first into the snow.

The Dowager Countess had begun to fill her plate from the fresh dishes that had been placed in front of them as if nothing untoward was taking place. Sarah was still giggling into her napkin as if the situation was something to laugh at. Therefore it was down to Cressida to smooth things over.

'My lord, Papa, you are making cakes of yourselves. Sit down and stop behaving like a pair of schoolboys squabbling over a bag of marbles.' Both of them turned to her, and if looks could kill she would have been dead twice over. 'Papa, you can hardly throw Lord Bromley out in such inclement weather — he would perish within hours. My lord, you and your family have no choice but to stay here at least until after the festive season. Don't you think it would be sensible to sit down and resume your dinner, and we will all pretend this incident never took place?'

Her sister was now following her ladyship's lead and helping herself to the delicious removes that had been fetched in. Cressida pointed to a dish of buttered leeks that was in front of Bromley. 'Would you be so kind as to serve me from that plate, my lord? For I am very partial to leeks.'

Her father sat down and began a conversation with Lady Bromley, leaving his lordship little choice but to follow suit. He stared at her and she didn't look away. 'I should be delighted to help you, Miss Hadley.' He proceeded to pile an inordinate amount of vegetables on and then passed the laden plate back.

'Thank you, my lord. Would you care for some lobster patties?'

He nodded and handed her his plate, and she was tempted to give him all twelve, but decided this wouldn't be fair on the others who had yet to help themselves from this delicacy. 'How many would you like?'

'One will be sufficient, thank you, as I have no wish to deprive others of the treat.' There was a decided twinkle in his eyes, and she was beginning to enjoy the exchange.

'Are you implying, sir, that my partiality for buttered leeks is unacceptable?'

'Not at all. I'm eager to see you eat them, for there's nothing I like better than a young lady with a healthy appetite.'

Cressida caught the eye of a lurking footman and indicated she would like a clean plate. This appeared immediately, and with commendable aplomb she removed a couple of leeks and transferred them to her clean one. Guy's deep, attractive chuckle immediately attracted everyone's attention.

The Dowager Countess smiled benignly. 'Well done, Miss Hadley. You have somehow managed to restore Bromley's good humour, and now we may relax and enjoy the remainder of this delightful dinner.'

Sarah also joined in the conversation, and soon the badinage was light-hearted and no longer acrimonious. However, Cressida was sure that Papa and Bromley had taken a dislike of each other; and, if this was not to be a disastrous Christmas, she must try and keep them apart. She hoped her brother would be able to join them tomorrow, as for all his rackety ways, he was easy-going and slow to take offence. He would be able to stand between the older gentlemen and hopefully prevent any further disagreements.

Tonight would not be a good time to leave the men to their port whilst the ladies retired to the drawing room. 'I thought I would play you a selection of tunes suitable for this time of year, and then you could all join in,' Cressida suggested. 'As I wish to check on both my patients before retiring, I think it would be sensible to decline your port this evening, Papa.'

It wasn't the colonel who stood up, but the earl. He moved smoothly around the table and whisked his mother from her chair before her father could object. 'Come along, Mama. You know how you love to sing.'

Cressida and Sarah were close behind, and this left the colonel no option but to follow, albeit with bad grace. He expected things to be done in the time-honoured way, and foregoing his port, even this once, did not sit happily with him.

The pianoforte was at the far end of the spacious chamber and Cressida hurried towards it. There was no need for her to search for music, as she only intended to play songs that she knew. 'I shall play 'Hark! The Herald Angels Sing' and other such songs, and you must all join in.'

When she ran out of festive tunes,

she played 'Greensleeves', and Sarah and Bromley's rendition of this traditional song was quite exceptional. Lady Bromley had fallen asleep, and the colonel had stomped off to his study, saying that he had no interest in such frivolity.

After an hour, Cressida closed the piano lid and stood up. 'Shall we wake your mama so we can help her upstairs?' she asked Guy.

He shook his head. 'I'll carry her to her room. It won't be the first time I've done so, and it certainly won't be the last.' Without further ado, he scooped his mother from her chair and strode off as if she weighed nothing at all.

Sarah yawned. 'That was a most enjoyable evening, especially the fracas in the dining room. I know that it's not fashionable to decorate the house or make a fuss at Christmas, but as we have house guests for the first time in living memory, do you think we could make an exception this year?'

'I think I have no option if we are to

keep Papa and Bromley from fisticuffs. There's three days until Christmas Eve — plenty of time to gather greenery from the woods and make garlands. I can remember Grandpapa telling me that in the old days they had parlour games, performed pantomimes, and there was something special on every one of the twelve days of Christmas. This year we shall do the same.'

'Our grand guests will still be here when we hold our New Year ball. My word, won't our neighbours be impressed to see an actual earl in residence.'

'Indeed they will, my love,' Cressida agreed, 'and I'm looking forward to it already. If I'm to be involved with garland-making and so on, could I rely on you to entertain Lord Harry once he's able to hobble to a daybed in his sitting room?'

'You certainly can. I find Lord Bromley somewhat intimidating, and it's not just because he is of such a prodigious size. You've already met

Lord Harry — is he anything like his older brother?'

'Not at all. Lord Harry looks like Lady Bromley and Lady Amanda and has their friendly temperament as well — he's not at all like the earl.'

They strolled arm in arm through the drawing room and out into the hall. The wall sconces were left burning until Grimshaw retired, and this wouldn't be until all the family were safely in bed, so there was no necessity to carry a candle. Cressida took this opportunity to tell her sister the dreadful news about Richard. Sarah was remarkably sanguine about the whole affair.

'You refine on this too much, Cressie. Richard's always getting into trouble, but he charms his way out of it, and Papa will forgive him yet again. It's not as if there isn't the money to pay his gambling debts.'

'I hope you're right, my love. I intend to take the guest stairs, as I'm going to visit both patients before going to bed. I hope Papa's in a better humour tomorrow, but I doubt he will be when he hears about Richard. It's not just the money; that gelding was his favourite.'

Her sister laughed. 'Actually, Cressie, I think the next three weeks will be far more fun if the earl and Papa are at loggerheads. Having Richard stir the pot will just make it more enjoyable. Imagine our own parent behaving badly — we shall dine out on it for months.'

★　★　★

Guy kicked open the bedchamber door and deposited his mother unceremoniously upon her bed. Her maid curtsied and waited politely for him to retreat. 'Lady Bromley has imbibed too much champagne,' he said unnecessarily.

Although alcohol went to her head, his mama never refused a glass of wine if it was offered, and left it to him to take care of the consequences. For this reason, alcohol was rarely served at dinner at Bromley Court.

The hour was early, too soon to

retire, but Guy could hardly remain downstairs when he was *persona non grata* with his host. He would visit his brother and entertain him with the ridiculous events that had taken place at the dinner table. He could reach the downstairs apartment without the necessity of venturing into the main part of the building.

Harry's sitting room was lit only by a substantial fire, but this was sufficient for Guy to see his way across to the bedchamber door. He pushed it open and stepped quietly inside. He was unsurprised, but disappointed, to see his brother sleeping soundly. There was a second figure slumped in a chair next to the bed with a blanket draped across his knees — this must be the temporary valet.

Satisfied everything was as it should be, Guy returned to the sitting room. From the brief time he'd spent in his own apartment, he'd observed that although well-appointed, the *escritoire* held neither paper nor pens. He must write to his uncle and inform him of the accident. Also, arrangements would have to be made to remove his ruined carriage. He had another suitable vehicle at home, and this must be brought to him, but there was no urgency as they wouldn't be going anywhere until Harry was able to travel without doing further damage to his broken leg.

As he was collecting the items he needed to write his letters, Miss Hadley walked in and failed to see him in the semi-darkness. Something prompted him to remain silent until she'd checked on her patient and come out, closing the door quietly behind her. As she moved into the room, he spoke: 'Good evening, Miss Hadley.'

She appeared to leap several inches from the floor, and he couldn't hold back his shout of laughter. What was the matter with him tonight? He had almost got himself evicted from the Abbey, and now was indulging in silly games.

'Bromley, have you run mad? I almost had an apoplexy. What are you doing lurking in the shadows and playing pranks like a schoolboy?'

He moved into the firelight and waved the items he'd been collecting. 'I have missives to write but not the wherewithal in my own rooms.' He bowed and smiled, hoping this might charm her into forgiving him. 'As you might imagine, I'm not eager to risk meeting the colonel again tonight.'

'Very wise, my lord. My father won't hesitate to floor you if you annoy him again. I took you for a sensible and sober gentleman when first we met, but I now realise I was quite mistaken. I sincerely hope that your siblings are not as giddy as you.' She dipped in a graceful curtsy and he bowed a second time.

'I can only apologise for my intemperate behaviour. I'm renowned for my good sense and propriety, and have never played a prank in my life before tonight. There must be something very unusual about this place to cause such a change in my character.'

Finally Cressida smiled. 'Indeed, sir, this place is not known for frivolity or japes of any kind. Until the unexpected arrival of you and your family, we were set for a subdued festive season as always, and now all that has changed.'

He gestured to a pair of matching armchairs positioned on either side of the fire. 'Shall we be seated, Miss Hadley, and I'll find some candles? It's some time since I have conversed with a young lady in the dark.'

Her slight gasp at his words made him pause. What the devil? Then he understood she thought him to be referring to bedroom sport. 'Tarnation take it. Do you think me so unmannerly to . . . to . . . ' He was floundering, not sure how to proceed without making matters worse. He spluttered to a halt.

'Do go on, my lord. I cannot wait to hear exactly why you thought I inadvertently gasped.'

She was enjoying his discomfiture,

and this cleared his head. 'You were no doubt under the erroneous impression that I was talking about my mistress, but I can assure I was not.'

'Good grief! I thought no such thing. Who do you take me for? My shocked reaction was because I thought you might have once played a parlour game that involved dousing the candles.' She was on her feet and staring down at him with disapproval. 'I'm not sure which offends me most — that you believed I could think of something so indelicate, or that you felt it permissible to refer to your mistress in my presence.' She turned on her heel and stalked out, leaving him in no doubt that this round of hostilities had gone in her favour.

He stretched out his legs towards the fire and sighed loudly. What in hell's name was wrong with him? He was famous for his set-downs; no young buck or dizzy debutante had ever had the temerity to offend him. His friends and acquaintances held him in high respect. Yet in this establishment he had been laughed at, threatened with violence, and given a bear-garden jaw by a young lady ten years his junior, and all in the space of a few hours.

This enforced visit was certainly going to be interesting, but he was determined to gain the ascendancy and put the redoubtable Miss Hadley firmly in her place. For some reason, he was no longer keen to pay court to her delectable sister, despite the indisputable fact that Miss Sarah made her older sibling look both dowdy and plain.

5

Cressida rose at six o'clock. The room was icy, as her fire had gone out during the night. She didn't expect Polly to attend her until seven, and she had no intention of ringing for her so early. There were sufficient embers beneath the ashes to kindle a candle, however; and by the light of this flickering flame she pulled on a serviceable but warm gown and added thick stockings and sturdy footwear.

Once she was dressed, she pulled back the curtain and one shutter. She gazed out of her bedroom window to see what the night had brought. There was sufficient moonlight to see that at least twelve inches of snow had fallen overnight, although thankfully the storm had now passed over. This meant it was extremely unlikely that the Bromley luggage cart and their personal servants would be appearing today, which was a nuisance. However, as this would also mean the men dunning her brother for unpaid gambling debts would also be unable to get to the Abbey, she was pleased they were snowed in.

The kitchen maids and junior parlourmaids would be up preparing breakfast and scrubbing floors, so the kitchen would be warm. Perhaps she could make herself a hot drink before going to the attics and finding suitable garments for the earl.

There was an oil lamp in her sitting room, and Cressida decided that would be far easier to carry and give better light. As she walked past her sister's chamber, she decided this task would be less onerous with her to help in the search. No one locked their chamber doors at the Abbey, so she quietly stepped into Sarah's bedroom and was unsurprised to find the bed empty. A faint glimmer coming from beneath the dressing-room door meant her sister was about her ablutions.

'Sarah, I need your assistance. We have to find our unwanted guests something to wear until their own garments arrive.'

The cheerful voice replied from within, 'I shall be ready in a few minutes. Has there been more snow?'

'Indeed there has, my love, and the lanes will be quite impassable for days.'

Whilst she was waiting, Cressida found a second oil lamp and removed the glass in order to light the wick. Together the sisters made their way to the end of the corridor and took the much narrower staircase, which led to the attics.

'Good grief, Sarah, it's perishing up here. We should have put on our cloaks and mufflers. Can you remember where the trunks with the discarded garments were put?'

'I believe they were placed with the boxes and packing-cases that came from India. Imagine, our very own grandmother travelled so far away. I should love to go there — no snow or freezing weather like this to endure.'

Cressida was having difficulty stopping her teeth from chattering. 'On balance, I think I prefer our more temperate weather. And I've no desire to meet a snake or tiger, but I should like to see an elephant.'

This was a ridiculous conversation to be having with her sister, but it took her mind off her numb extremities. Fortunately it was possible for both of them to walk upright as long as they remained in the centre of the attic.

'Look, Sarah — I recognise that trunk. I helped Mama pack it ten years ago. I'm certain we've found what we want.'

The object was too heavy for them to carry, but they dragged it into the centre of the room so that the footmen could collect it later and take it to his lordship. His temporary valet could have the unenviable task of rummaging through and finding items that might be suitable.

'I seem to recall that our grandfather was taller than Papa, but I don't believe he was anywhere near as wide in the shoulders as the earl.' Cressida was feeling slightly warmer after their exertions and was eager to discover the trunk they needed for Lady Bromley.

'I thought that aristocrats were by their very nature thin and ascetic-looking, so how is it that Lord Bromley is so massive?' Sarah had flung open a second trunk, but this contained bolts of exotic materials and wasn't what they were looking for.

As the lid slammed shut, Cressida changed her mind. 'I think we should have this taken down to the sewing room. Indian silks and cottons are highly prized, and perhaps we could find something suitable to give to Lady Bromley and Lady Amanda as a Christmas gift'

This too was manoeuvred into the centre of the attic. After a further half-hour of rummaging, they discovered the trunks they sought, and could now return to the warmth of the lower floors.

The house was still quiet, the sconces unlit, and the shutters and curtains remained drawn. 'I am famished and frozen to the marrow, Sarah, and I'm going to the kitchen to find a hot drink and something to eat. Are you coming with me?'

Her sister nodded. 'I am indeed. However, Cressie, I think we had better do something about our appearance before we descend, just in case any of our guests are early risers. You have cobwebs in your hair and several smuts on your face.'

'And you are not much better. Your chamber is nearer, so we shall repair the damage there.'

They brushed the worst of the debris from their garments and washed their hands and faces.

'I really think we should take some time to change our gowns, for the hem of mine is coming down and yours is as bad,' Cressida said.

'Fiddlesticks to that! This is our home; we can appear as we wish. And if any of our guests see us and take umbrage, I care not for that.' Sarah grabbed her sister's arm and gave her no opportunity to disagree. They were breathless and laughing when they reached the vestibule. The remaining pins in Cressida's hair slid out and it tumbled over her shoulders.

'Botheration! I look like a hoyden. But it's too cold here to repair the damage. You can help me put it up again when we're in the warmth of the kitchen.' Only then did she become aware they were no longer alone.

'Good morning, Miss Hadley, Miss Sarah. I am in search of sustenance. Is it too early to ring for coffee?'

Cressida gripped her sister's hand like a lifeline and stared at the earl with horror. For all their brave words about not caring who saw them in torn and besmirched gowns, she was mortified to be seen as she was.

Somehow she regained the use of her

tongue. 'Breakfast is usually served at nine o'clock, my lord; but if you would care to wait in the yellow drawing room, I shall see if something can be done immediately.'

He smiled and looked almost friendly. His eyes were so dark the black centres were indistinguishable, and his teeth so white he reminded her of the wolf in the Red Riding Hood fairytale.

'Forgive me, Miss Hadley, but I could not but help overhear you saying you and your sister are heading for the kitchen. Would you allow me to accompany you? I shall surely freeze to death if you leave me here.'

As he was as warmly dressed as they, and looked as robust as a prize bull, this eventuality was highly unlikely. 'Cook would have hysterics if we invaded her sanctum with a member of the aristocracy in tow. Sarah, would you go for us and have whatever is ready sent to the breakfast parlour?'

Her sister ran off, leaving her alone

with her disconcerting companion. 'The fires are laid everywhere, but they will not be lit,' she said. 'I intend to remedy this, as I take it someone as toplofty as yourself would find it demeaning to light a fire.'

Her provocative comment had the desired effect. 'I have a candle and am quite capable of using it.' He strode off into the grand drawing room and she left him to it.

By the time the fire in the breakfast parlour was burning fiercely, Cressida had visited the study and the library and ignited the kindling. Her hands were now in need of washing, so she would be obliged to quickly return to her chamber.

★ ★ ★

Guy resented any suggestion that he was too feeble-minded to be able to light a fire without calling for a servant. Miss Hadley was under the mistaken impression that he never got his hands dirty and was incapable of doing anything practical.

There were two substantial fireplaces in the drawing room, and it was the work of minutes to get both fires burning merrily. He waited until they were fully ignited in order to be able to add logs and coal. Satisfied they would stay alight until the parlourmaid arrived, he wandered to one of the mullioned windows and pulled back the curtains and opened the shutters.

Although it was barely dawn, the snow made it brighter than it should be at seven o'clock in late December. Nothing would get through to them today, possibly not for a week, unless there was a thaw. This was a damned nuisance, as he would now have to wear borrowed clothes, and he doubted that there was anything large enough for him. He would be a figure of fun in jackets that wouldn't fit across his shoulders and breeches that were too short to tuck into his boots. There was no point in dwelling on this, however, as the situation could have been far worse. At least his family had come out of a nasty carriage accident relatively unscathed. Also, the Abbey was a luxurious, well-run establishment, and if it wasn't for his objectionable host he might actually enjoy the experience of staying here.

He checked his hands for coal dust and was pleased to see he'd managed to light the fires without becoming mired himself. He'd no idea of the where-abouts of this breakfast parlour, but hopefully there would be a servant about their duties he could ask.

As he made his way down the length of the room, he smiled as he recalled his second lively exchange with Miss Hadley. For some reason, she was prejudiced against him and thought him arrogant and proud. He was a peer of the realm, a wealthy man with substantial investments and estates, so it was only to be expected that he held himself in high esteem. It was a salutary experience to discover that not everyone he met was of the same opinion.

As he emerged from the drawing room, the bad-tempered butler slid around the corner. The man bowed. 'My lord, I shall conduct you to the breakfast parlour, where Miss Hadley and Miss Sarah are waiting for you.'

He made it sound as if Guy had been dawdling deliberately and not doing the bidding of his mistress. He merely nodded and didn't deign to reply.

The breakfast parlour proved to be a snug chamber in the east wing. The two girls were inspecting the chafing dishes and barely bothered to acknowledge Guy's arrival.

'Lord Bromley, shall we turn etiquette on its head again this morning?' Miss Hadley asked with a charming smile. 'If you care to be seated, Sarah and I will fetch you what you want.' She then listed what was on offer, and he was impressed that so much could have been prepared so quickly. He took his seat and poured himself a cup of coffee from the silver pot in the centre of the table. He was inordinately fond of this aromatic brew and took it without cream or sugar.

'Here you are, sir,' Cressida said. 'Crisply fried ham from our own pigs, eggs from our chickens, and fried potatoes from our fields. Sarah is bringing you butter for your toast.'

'From your cows?'

'Of course, but I am sad to inform you that contrary to your expectations, our dairy herd is unable to produce butter — therefore we are obliged to churn it ourselves.'

'You are quite outrageous, my dear, and over the next few weeks I shall make it my business to demonstrate to you that your opinion of me is incorrect.'

'Few weeks? I had no idea you were intending to make such an extended stay, my lord. How fortunate our house is big enough to accommodate everyone. No doubt your servants will arrive eventually and also require to be fed and housed.'

He bit back his sharp retort. Her comment was bordering on damn rude, and there was no call for her to be so uncivil. He daren't look at her, as he was sure his anger would be apparent in his expression. He took a mouthful or two of his breakfast before he looked up.

The wretched chit had turned back to the buffet, and was happily filling her plate and chatting to her sister about decorating the house with garlands and ribbons or some such nonsense. He was about to take her to task when the door opened, and to his surprise his sister and young Hadley wandered in.

To his certain knowledge, Amanda had never got up so early in her life before. His well-ordered world was shifting beneath his feet and he wasn't comfortable with the thought. He stood, as was expected when a gentleman or a lady came into the room, and nodded at her companion and smiled at his sister. 'Whatever has brought you down so early, Amanda? It's scarcely seven o'clock.'

She smiled sunnily. 'Like you, I woke up ravenously hungry. I can't remember the last time I ate. The broth I was given last night doesn't count.'

Miss Hadley immediately put down her own plate, and was about to hand his sister one, but Hadley was there before her.

'Allow me to serve you, Lady Amanda. If you would care to be seated, I'll bring it to you. Is there anything in particular you would like?'

'I'll have whatever is there, thank you, sir.' She joined him at the table and pointed to the larger silver jug. 'Is that chocolate? If it is, would you be kind enough to pour me a cup, Bromley?'

After a deal of chatter and fuss, eventually the entire party was seated and happily munching through the delicious repast. By the time he was replete, Guy had recovered his good humour and was ready to join in the friendly badinage.

'I should be happy to join in the expedition to gather ivy, holly and other suitable greenery,' he said. 'I assume you have woodland nearby, Hadley.' He thought it wiser not to address the prickly Miss Hadley directly. God knew why she'd taken him in dislike, as usually young ladies flocked about him and hung on his every word.

If he had announced he'd become a devil-worshipper, he could not have caused his sibling to look more shocked. 'You wish to trudge through the snow, Bromley, to get muddy and dirty and cold? I'm astonished, as I've never known you to put yourself out in such a way before.'

'That is because, my dear girl, the occasion has never arisen. Bromley Court has never been decorated for the festive season, so there has been no necessity to gather evergreens.'

Amanda snorted inelegantly and her chocolate slopped onto the tablecloth. 'You are doing it too brown, brother.

Even if we had done so, you would have sent an army of servants to collect what we needed and not become involved yourself.'

He raised his hand in surrender. 'Thank you for pointing this out to everybody at the table, Amanda. However, as you have brought the subject up, might I enquire, Miss Hadley, why you do not get your servants to do the collecting?'

'Actually, my lord, this house hasn't been decorated since our grandmother departed this earth many years ago,' Cressida replied. 'I do recall going out with a cart to gather greenery, but I couldn't have been more than ten years old. Grandmother loved to see the Abbey gaily dressed for the night before the Lord's name day. I wish to replicate those happy days, and as we have such a prestigious family staying with us, I believe Papa will not put a stop to it this year as he has on previous occasions when it's been suggested.'

Now Guy understood. 'I shall make

it very clear that I expect my every whim to be satisfied. And I will be most disagreeable if this establishment is not festooned with garlands and ribbons.' He was warming to his theme. 'Indeed, Miss Hadley, I insist that we have a yule log and play parlour games and perform a pantomime.'

Her smile was reward enough for embroiling himself in her plans. 'Lord Bromley, I shall convey your demands immediately my father is up. I'm sure he'll be delighted to accommodate your every wish, especially as he holds you in such high regard.' She said this with a straight face but was unable to maintain it.

The others watched them in bemusement as he and Miss Hadley collapsed into uncontrollable laughter. He spluttered to a stop and wiped his eyes on his napkin. 'I'd no idea breaking one's fast could be so jolly,' he said. 'On a more serious note, Miss Hadley, I've no intention of being a financial burden to this house. I shall have a banker's draft sent as soon as it can be arranged to cover our expenses.'

This time *she* looked uncomfortable, and her cheeks coloured. 'There's no need for that, my lord. I was being deliberately difficult and quite beyond the pale when I mentioned such a thing. I hope you can forgive me, and I promise to curb my tongue in future.'

'As I've said before, you are quite outrageous, but do not change on my account. I believe it will be quite entertaining to see you attempt to push me from my pedestal.'

6

Lord Harry was wide awake and eager to get out of bed when Cressida made her first visit that morning. 'I'm afraid that you must remain stationary for at least another three days, my lord, if you don't wish to have a permanent limp.'

He frowned, looking remarkably like his older brother. 'I shall go mad with boredom if I'm to be trapped here. I've never spent a day in bed in my life — I'm an active sort of fellow and don't take much to reading and that sort of thing.'

'Do you like playing cards?'

His expression changed and he grinned. 'What gentleman doesn't? I'll play anything as long as there's a wager in it.' He shifted on the bed and winced. 'However, I would prefer to play piquet or *vingt-et-un*.'

'In which case, I'll send my brother

up to you, as Richard is equally besotted with such pastimes. However, no money will be staked, you must gamble with buttons.'

'I feel much better now, Miss Hadley, and will be able to endure my incarceration if I can indulge in my passion. I'm a notable whipster and have won several races in my curricle as well as on horseback.'

'I dare say you will have plenty to talk about with my brother. You'll be pleased to know that your sister is fully recovered, and no doubt she will call in to see you later on as well.'

She left him chatting to his valet and was sanguine he would remain in bed at least for the next couple of days. After that, she believed it would be safe to have him carried to his sitting room, and then it would be permissible for Sarah to visit.

A second snowstorm had drifted in, and there was no possibility of taking the house party out in search of evergreens today. It also meant she could temporarily forget about the arrival of the men seeking Richard, which was a profound relief.

The trunks of clothes had been delivered and were being investigated by their respective servants. The thought of either Lady Bromley or her eldest son appearing in borrowed clothes was not a happy one. However, there was nothing that could be done about it, and they must make the best of the situation.

Sarah and Lady Amanda were of similar build and height, and the two of them were already closeted together sorting out suitable ensembles. Although Sarah was as casual about her appearance as Cressida was, they both owned a prodigious number of gowns, as this was one thing the colonel insisted upon. On the infrequent occasions when they entertained or attended neighbourhood events, he wished his family to look smart and fashionable as was appropriate for one of the wealthiest men in the county.

As Cressida was about to leave, she heard Lady Bromley cry out. Although her chambers were a goodly distance from the gallery where Cressida was standing, the sound carried. What disaster had overtaken the Bromley family now?

She gathered up her skirts and ran pell-mell, bursting into the sitting room without pausing to knock. Her ladyship was crouched over a trunk and shrieking with excitement. Surely Mama's garments could not have elicited such a response. 'Lady Bromley, I heard you calling out and came immediately to see if I could render any assistance.'

The lady sat back on her heels and held up a length of beautiful embroidered silk. 'My dear, where did all this exquisite material come from? Do you have seamstresses who can cut and sew?'

Botheration! The footmen had delivered the wrong trunk, and now all their precious Indian material appeared to belong to Lady Bromley. She summoned up a happy smile. 'These bolts of material were bought by my grandmother, who travelled extensively before she was married.'

'And you have never had it made up? I'm sure you didn't intend me to have this trunk — the second one with old-fashioned but expensive items was obviously meant for me.'

Cressida felt ashamed she had immediately assumed the worst. 'To be honest, my lady, I'd forgotten it was up there until this morning. Polly and Jane, the girls who take care of my sister and me, are experts with the needle and can also cut a pattern.'

She dropped to her knees beside Lady Bromley and together they examined the contents. 'There's more than enough to make all of us a special gown for the festive season. I'll go and find my sister and Lady Amanda and we can select the cloth we want.'

'How exciting — my daughter is *au fait* with current fashions and could sketch designs for us. Do you think your girls would be able to work from that?'

Cressida jumped to her feet. 'I'm certain they can. Although we employ a modiste from London when we do a major refurbishment of our wardrobes, when we want a single item or two they copy the latest fashion plates in *La Belle Assemblée* with no difficulty.'

She was about to offer her hand to assist her ladyship to her feet, but her help wasn't needed. 'I quite forgot,' Lady Bromley said, 'as I was so giddy with excitement on seeing these treasures, but I owe you my sincerest apology for my appalling behaviour last night. I know alcohol does not agree with me, but time and time again I cannot resist. Bromley is constantly on edge when we're out in case I become inebriated.'

This apology was made so sincerely that Cressida warmed to the lady. 'You must behave as if you were at home, my lady. We have no wish to make any of you uncomfortable whilst you're snow-bound here.'

Before she could step away, she was embraced and soundly kissed on each cheek. The Hadleys were not a demonstrative family, and such open displays of feeling were unheard of. Strangely, however, Cressida rather enjoyed the experience of being hugged, and tentatively returned the gesture.

'To tell you the truth, my dear, I was rather dreading spending Christmas with my brother and his boisterous family. There are far too many of them and they are loud and far too jolly. Poor Bromley would have hated it, and only agreed that we should go because Harry and Amanda gave him no peace until he said yes.' Lady Bromley smiled knowingly. 'I believe it was fate that brought us here, and I couldn't be happier to spend the next few weeks in the company of you and your delightful family.'

The idea that the earl could be influenced in this way was food for thought. Although Cressida's personal experience of aristocrats was somewhat limited, she had read more than enough on the subject to believe she was well-informed. The earl was, in her considered opinion, the epitome of someone in such a position: arrogant and proud, and so accustomed to getting his own way that it wouldn't occur to him that anyone else's opinion could be of any value.

'Well, apart from the fact that your youngest son has broken his leg, I'm also pleased you arrived unexpectedly on our doorstep,' Cressida said. 'My father doesn't enjoy frivolity, and believes that Christmas is a time for reflection and celebration of Christ's birth, not a time for gaiety and fun. However, this year it shall be different, and the house will come alive.'

'Run along and fetch the girls, then,' said Lady Bromley with a grin. 'I'll lay out the materials so we can make a proper choice. Perhaps you could ask your abigail to come as well?'

Sarah and her new friend had abandoned their search for suitable garments and were curled up in front of the fire, discussing the weather, when Cressida arrived. 'Girls, you must come at once with me as I have a surprise for you. Lady Amanda — '

'Please, would you drop the formality and call me by my given name? Sarah and I are now on familiar terms, and I would love to be the same with you.'

Surprised but pleased, Cressida nodded. 'And you must call me Cressie, as my siblings do. I'm sure that your brother will enjoy being addressed in future by his given name.'

Her comment had been intended as a joke, but Amanda gasped and her colour faded. 'Oh, you must not do that. He is a stickler for protocol, and no one, not even his family, ever use his given name.'

'I was funning, Amanda. I wouldn't dream of being so presumptuous.

Anyway, I've no idea what his name is.'

'The first of his many names is Guy — but no one would dare to address him by it.'

As she led the two girls back to the guest wing, Cressida mulled over what Amanda had said about her brother. She was determined to call him Guy at the earliest opportunity just to see his reaction. She thought that he might explode with indignation when she did so.

★   ★   ★

When Guy returned to his rooms after breakfast, he found that the garments he was expected to borrow had arrived in his absence.

Jones, his temporary valet, bowed. 'I have set out a selection of items for your perusal, my lord. They are rather old-fashioned, but of excellent cut and material.'

Guy gave the items a cursory glance and shook his head. 'I shall use the shirts, socks and hosiery but have no wish to walk around in a dead man's clothes. You have done wonders with my topcoat and breeches so far; no doubt you can continue to keep them looking pristine until my baggage arrives.'

His valet bowed and appeared satisfied with his reply. 'The trunk shall be removed immediately. I took your letters downstairs for the post, my lord, but they won't go today, that's for sure.'

'One of my grooms should be capable of taking them to the nearest post inn — he can ride a dray horse. I shall see to it myself.' He grabbed his riding coat, gloves and beaver, as he was going to need them if he intended to go outside.

He called in to see his brother and was satisfied that Harry was doing as well as could be expected. In fact, he seemed remarkably cheerful considering the circumstances. The place was warmer now that the parlourmaids had all the fires lit. If he was honest, the

Abbey was considerably warmer than Bromley Court, despite its age.

The butler appeared at his summons and immediately produced the letters he'd sent down earlier. 'It is snowing heavily again, my lord.'

The man was an imbecile. Only a blind person could fail to see that the weather had deteriorated. Guy ignored the comment and strode off in search of the side door he'd used yesterday. With his beaver pulled down over his ears, his coat buttoned up to the neck and his gloves on, he scarcely felt the cold.

Despite the flurries of snow, the stable yard was swept clean, and each loose box had an equine head peering over the door. Fred, his coachman, appeared like a genie from a bottle.

'Have the horses taken any harm from their experience yesterday?' Guy asked.

'No, my lord. They're fine.' He nodded towards the letters Guy produced from his inside pocket. 'I thought you might wish to send letters. Young

Tom is ready to go, and we've found a sturdy mount for him that won't mind a bit of snow and such.'

'Excellent. Could you also make enquiries as to the whereabouts of our baggage? If it's marooned in the village, then a diligence could be sent to collect both staff and trunks.'

Fred touched his cap. 'We was wondering, my lord, seeing as Lord Harry has broken his leg, are we likely to be staying here for a while?'

'I know it's a bore, but it can't be helped. My brother cannot travel for three weeks. Is your accommodation satisfactory?'

Fred nodded vigorously and a broad smile lit his face. 'It's grand, my lord, and the food's plentiful and hot. We eat in the servants' hall along with everyone else, not like some places where the outside staff are treated like dirt.'

'I'm glad to hear it. I assume that you and Tom are making yourself useful once our horses are taken care of?'

Assured that this was the case, Guy

returned to the house, where he was met by two diligent footmen. One removed his outdoor garments and handed them ceremoniously to the second before dropping to his knees in order to polish his boots.

'Thank you. Could you tell me, are the family down yet?'

The young man bounded to his feet. 'The master is in the breakfast parlour, my lord. The ladies are upstairs in Lady Bromley's apartment, and Mr Hadley is playing cards with Lord Harry.'

Guy nodded his thanks, relieved the colonel was safely ensconced with his breakfast. He wasn't ready for another confrontation so early in the day. He was at a loss to know how to fill his time — at home he would be busy reading the latest edition of the *Times* or going about estate business.

Not wishing to be caught lurking in the passageway, he decided to join his brother and young Hadley. It would probably be wise to oversee the card-playing and make sure neither of them was wagering real money on the outcome.

His arrival was greeted with enthusiasm by Harry, but Hadley looked rather dismayed and immediately stood up. 'I've no wish to intrude, my lord, so will make myself scarce.' Before Guy could prevent him, the young man shot off like a rat from a haystack with a terrier behind it.

Harry was less than pleased by this development. 'Dammit, Bromley, now look what you've done. Richard and I were enjoying a game of whist. He trounced me at *vingt-et-un*.'

Guy perched himself on the vacated chair by the bed. 'Why in the name of Hades did he rush off like that?'

'Because you're such an irascible fellow that no one wants to remain in your company for long in case they get one of your fulminating stares or a severe put-down for no reason at all.'

'Are you sure? I thought myself an amiable cove and had no notion I was universally disliked.'

'Don't overstate the matter, Bromley. I said you were not an easy man to talk to, not that people don't like you. I'm sure Richard will come round once he knows you better.' He pointed to the abandoned cards. 'As it's entirely your responsibility that I'm left without a partner, you must take his place and his hand.'

They spent an enjoyable hour, and then Harry wished to relieve himself and Guy had no intention of assisting with that. 'I expect your sister and mother will call in later on. I'll see if there are any journals in the library that I can fetch you, as I know there's no point in bringing you an actual book.'

He flicked open his gold pocket watch and saw the hour was approaching midday. Presumably the ladies would have refreshments, and he would join them as he had nothing better to do. What he needed was some exercise, but short of running up and down the stairs like a lunatic he could think of no other way to stretch his legs.

An impulse made him run up to his mother's apartment and knock on the sitting-room door. The door opened and a nervous maid curtsied and stepped aside to allow him to enter.

Guy looked around in wonder. The room had been transformed into an Indian bazaar — exotic materials, beads, bangles and gold embroidered ribbons were draped over every available surface. The four ladies were clustered about a table examining what looked like a pile of drawings of some sort.

Mama eventually looked up long enough to acknowledge him. 'Bromley, you are *de trop*. This is ladies' business and gentlemen are not wanted here.' This was said with a friendly smile and she gestured towards the kaleidoscope of materials. 'As you can see, we are busy choosing patterns for our celebration gowns.'

He was about to retreat when Cressida put down the paper she had been perusing and picked her way carefully through the silks, cottons and muslins until she arrived at his side. 'We are almost done here, my lord, and I am about to check on Lord Harry before we go down for refreshment. I hope you will join us? Luncheon is served in the small dining room, which you will find adjacent to the breakfast parlour.' She glided past him, narrowly avoiding treading on his toes.

'Like most gentlemen, I am usually busy with estate business and other matters at this time. However, I find myself hungry again, so will certainly be there.' Guy moved quickly so that he could walk beside her. 'I cannot imagine why this is so, as I ate far more than was good for me at breakfast.'

They had reached Harry's room, and Cressida knocked and was admitted. While he waited, Guy strolled up and down the spacious corridor, examining the many family portraits that hung in miserable rows down either side.

'They are dire, are they not, my lord?' Cressida asked; she had returned unnoticed, quietly shutting the door behind her. 'Papa has them in the guest wing; as it is so rarely used, few people are obliged to look at them.'

'I have dozens of similar monstrosities, but I have resorted to hiding them amongst more attractive pictures in the hope that they will be not be noticed. You must tell me if I have succeeded when you visit Bromley Court.'

God's teeth! He'd just invited her to visit his familial home. This was tantamount to expressing an interest in her, which could not be further from the case.

7

For a moment Cressida was speechless. Had she heard aright? How was she to respond to this casual invitation to visit at Bromley Court? Then her composure returned as she realised she had misinterpreted Guy's remark. Of course he was obligated to invite her family to visit in reciprocation for their enforced stay at the Abbey.

'We shall all look forward to coming in the summer, my lord. I'm sure we can manage a week with you at some point in our busy itinerary.'

'I shall leave my mother and yourself to arrange the details, Miss Hadley. However, I cannot promise to be at home myself, as I visit my northern estates when the weather is more clement.'

Cressida wasn't sure if she was offended or relieved that he was making it abundantly clear his invitation was not personal but merely good manners. 'Good heavens, I see that somebody has ridden down the drive this morning. I assume that you have sent one of your men to try and locate your baggage carriage.'

'Exactly so. I'm hoping they might not be too far away, but have had the sense to take shelter in the next village. If that is the case, then I'm hoping I can organise a farm cart to fetch our personal servants and our trunks.'

'Now that the snow has stopped and the sun is out, such a vehicle might well be able to traverse lanes that a normal carriage cannot.'

As they neared the central passageway downstairs, she detected a certain nervousness in her companion. She spoke without thinking how her words might be considered inflammatory. 'Papa never comes for luncheon, so you may relax, sir, as you will not be evicted this morning.'

Immediately she wished to stuff the

words back inside her mouth, but it was too late. She risked a glance in Guy's direction and was dismayed to see his expression. His monumental pride had been dented by her comment. Should she risk it? Some imp of mischief pushed her into further scandalous behaviour.

'I was teasing you, sir. I promise that my father will have forgotten all about your disagreement when you meet this evening. Now that our sisters have decided that our families are to be the best of friends, we shall no longer be formal when addressing each other. You have my permission to call me Cressida, and I shall call you Guy.' She smiled sweetly at him and waited for the explosion.

If it had been possible for him to grow any larger, then she was sure he would have done so, such was his fury at her impertinence. From his formidable height he raked her with an icy glare. 'You shall do no such thing. I am Lord Bromley to you and your family

— do I make myself quite clear?'

She refused to be intimidated in her own home. For the first time in her life, she was glad she was so tall, and merely by tilting her head she could meet his eyes. 'How silly of me to have thought you might wish to behave like a reasonable person for the first time in your life. You will, of course, remain Lord Bromley. As the rest of your family wish to be addressed informally, perhaps it would be better for you to dine in solitary splendour in future, my lord?'

Deciding that discretion was definitely the better part of valour, she picked up her skirts and walked rapidly away from him before he could reply. She reached the sanctuary of the small dining room and was delighted to find two footmen putting the finishing touches to the table.

The aromatic smell of vegetable soup wafted towards her from the large tureen sitting in the centre of the table. There was a plate of meat pasties, cold cuts and pickles as well as freshly baked bread and butter. Apple pie and a jug of thick cream waited on the sideboard for dessert.

* * *

Guy wanted to punch the wall, to vent his rage on something physical. God dammit to hell! How dare she speak to him like that? Never in his life had anyone had the temerity to use his given name. And yet . . . and yet. His anger evaporated like snow in the sunshine. After all, hadn't he dared Miss Hadley to attempt to push him off his pedestal? Having his position challenged like this was a new experience, and if he was honest, quite an invigorating one. He had been bemoaning the fact that he had nothing with which to occupy his time, and now everything had changed. The girl might well be expecting him to storm off in high dudgeon and remain aloof from the company, wallowing in his own superiority. However, if this was the case, she was going to be sadly disappointed.

He followed her down the corridor and into the dining room. 'If I am to eat alone, my dear Miss Hadley, then I must ask you to vacate this chamber. I shall let you know when I've finished my meal.'

At his words she spun so fast her skirts flew out, revealing not a trim ankle, but ugly outdoor boots. 'Have you run mad, sir? What nonsense are you talking now?'

He wasn't aware he'd been talking nonsense, but he decided not to argue the point. He bowed and stood to one side as if actually expecting her to leave. 'My dear Miss Hadley, do not tell me that I misunderstood your rather strident suggestion that I eat on my own in future?'

She all but stamped her foot, and he was having difficulty keeping a straight face. 'If you call me *your dear Miss Hadley* one more time, I'll not be answerable for the consequences.'

He was about to laugh and call it quits when her frown lifted and she fixed him with a basilisk stare. 'Actually, my lord, if you will recall exactly what I said, it was that you should *dine* alone — and as this is luncheon, the new arrangement does not apply.' She was beginning to look decidedly smug, and he feared he was going to lose this encounter. 'I shall arrange for you to have your dinner served in the main dining room, and we shall eat in comfort and relaxation in here.'

He had been hoisted by his own petard, and it served him right. If he didn't wish to spend the rest of his evenings in isolation, he'd better eat humble pie. 'I surrender. You have won this battle, Miss Hadley, but I can assure you the war is not yet over. I have no wish to eat on my own, as you very well know. What must I do to have you rescind your orders?'

She pouted and touched her fingertip to her lips as if considering the matter.

'Well, sir, I think that you must dismount from your very high horse and give me permission to address you as — '

He braced himself, knowing whatever the consequences, he could not possibly allow her to call him Guy.

' — Bromley, as your family does.'

He was so relieved that he agreed immediately, and they were able to converse without coming to daggers drawn whilst they awaited the arrival of the rest of the party.

Although she had been given permission to drop his title, Cressida was reluctant to do so, as she felt the concession had been rather grudging. Fortunately Richard and the ladies arrived at that moment, and the necessity to address Guy at all was removed.

'We are very informal here, so please be seated wherever you wish,' Cressida said. 'Then we just help ourselves. There is porter, small beer and lemonade on the sideboard for those who want it. Coffee is served at the end of the meal.'

'As always, Cressida, I am impressed by your efficiency.' Bromley raised an aristocratic eyebrow in her direction but kept a remarkably straight face.

'Bromley — I never thought to see the day when you . . . when you spoke so informally to a young lady,' his mother exclaimed.

Amanda dropped the soup ladle into the tureen and the liquid shot out in all directions, liberally coating her own hand and Richard's. 'Fiddlesticks! Now look what you've made me do. I do apologise, sir, for splashing you.'

By the time they were all sitting, harmony was restored; and apart from a few curious glances in Cressida's direction from Lady Bromley, no more was said. Cressida allowed her nerves to settle before she returned the favour. 'Bromley, would you be so kind as to pass me a slice of bread?'

He nodded solemnly. 'It will be my pleasure, Cressida. Would you care for a meat pasty as well?'

'No thank you, just the bread.'

He placed this with due ceremony on her plate, and then she was almost sure he winked at her. She snatched up her napkin and held it over her face in a vain attempt to prevent her laughter escaping.

Richard, who was sitting adjacent to her at the end of the table, put down his cutlery with a clatter. 'There's something havey-cavey going on here. Cut rope, Cressie. Stop sniggering behind your napkin and explain.'

Her brother looked quite put out, and this just made her laughter worse. She shook her head and nodded in Bromley's direction. He rose to the occasion valiantly, although he too was having difficulty containing his amusement. 'Hadley,' he began, 'as the rest of you have agreed to informality, we decided we must attempt to do the same. However, I drew the line at being called by my given name and we settled for Bromley.'

Lady Bromley clapped her hands. 'How delightful! In future I shall be known as Aunt Elizabeth. I've not heard my name used since I was at home.'

'We would be honoured to call you thus,' Cressida managed to splutter. 'However, I don't think it would be wise for my father to be addressed as Uncle John. He would have a conniption fit.'

The luncheon continued in high spirits, and even Bromley joined in with the banter. They retired to the small drawing room for coffee. 'It looks quite magical out there with the sun reflecting on the snow and the sky so blue.' Sarah had been gazing through the window but now turned in excitement. 'I know it's deep, but could we not go out and build a snowman or two? I've not done that since I was in the schoolroom.'

As her sister cordially disliked being cold and wet, Cressida was somewhat surprised at this suggestion. Richard,

on the other hand, responded enthusiastically.

'I'm game — even if nobody else
wants to help you.'

Amanda shook her head. 'I promised
I would finish the designs for our gowns
this afternoon.'

Guy moved in beside Cressida, rather
too close for comfort. 'And you? Are
you going to brave the elements and
assist in the building of a snowman?'

She tilted her head and sent him a
challenging glance. 'I shall do so only if
you accompany us.' She was banking on
the fact that he would find such a
childish pastime too far beneath his
dignity, as she had absolutely no desire
to go outside.

'I can think of nothing better than
frolicking in the freezing cold with you,
my dear.' This was spoken so softly that
no one else would have heard his words.

If she didn't know better, she would
think he was flirting with her. She
stepped away hastily and joined her
siblings. 'We shall need spades, a

selection of vegetables, and a cap, gloves and muffler.' Guy looked mystified by her suggestion and she smiled at him. 'I take it this is the first time you will have made a snowman.'

'I'm ashamed to admit that it is. I understand the need for spades — but what of the rest of the items on your list?'

She explained the necessity for them as they were drinking their coffee. The footman who had brought the tray was sent in search of the list. Half an hour later, Cressida was warmly dressed and ready to go. Richard held the box with carrots and potatoes and Bromley had the spades. Sarah was carrying an old scarf, a cap and a pair of gloves with two fingers missing.

Richard took charge. 'I think the best place to build this snowman is by the turning circle, so we can see it from the drawing-room windows. So we'll go out through the front door — we don't want to trudge through more snow than we have to.'

'How big is this snowman going to be?' Guy asked.

'Two yards high,' Richard answered, 'so he can be seen by anyone who turns into the drive. Bromley, I'll explain to you how we go about this task, as my sisters have done it before. Cressie, you and Sarah start making the head, and we will do the first ball for the trunk.' He drew Guy to one side, and they were soon out of earshot.

Cressida stared after them. 'This is all very mysterious, Sarah. I've never known either you or Richard wish to build snowmen before.'

'Richard wished to speak to Bromley in private, and this was the only way he could think of doing so without being overheard by a member of staff who would report to Papa.'

'That explains it — but how did he know the earl would agree to come out? The whole enterprise was a trifle risky, if you want my opinion.'

Sarah was unable to reply as she fell flat on her face. 'Up you come,'

Cressida laughed. 'Let me brush you down. You could very well pass as the snow-woman at the moment.'

Before long, they had rolled a snowball of suitable proportions to go on a giant snowman. 'Shall we begin another one whilst we wait for the gentlemen to return?' Cressida pointed to the two figures that were doing more talking than rolling.

'My boots are filled with the wretched stuff,' Sarah complained, 'and my fingers are numb to the bone. I think we have been out here quite long enough, and we shall leave Richard and Bromley to complete the structure.'

'Agreed. I think I'll send round a couple of outside men to help them finish, or they will be here until dark.' As Cressida was turning away, she spotted a horseman turning into the drive. She pointed in excitement. 'Look! I do believe that's our Bessie. The rider must be someone from here.'

'He must have been sent with messages. No doubt Bromley would wish to inform his family of the accident and arrange for another carriage to come when the weather has improved.'

They headed for the side door, not wishing to track snow across the pristine floor of the grand entrance hall. A parlourmaid was waiting to take their snow-covered outer garments, and she handed the sisters a rag each to scrub away the worst of the slush from their boots.

They ran upstairs, and Cressida followed Sarah into her apartment. 'Richard must have been speaking to Bromley about his gambling debts,' said the former. 'I sincerely hope he's not trying to borrow money from him.'

'Richard could hardly speak to Papa about it, as he knows he will be packed off to the colonies or forced to join the East India Company if his gambling becomes common knowledge.'

'That's beside the point, Sarah. Our brother is a grown man, and it's high time he took responsibility for his own actions. He has a generous allowance and will inherit all this when Papa dies.'

'As our father is as fit as a flea and only in his late forties, it's unlikely Richard will inherit anything for many years to come.'

Cressida thought for a moment. 'I'm certain there is an estate somewhere in Derbyshire that Richard already holds in his own name — I'll suggest that he takes himself down there to rusticate. I doubt that anyone would find him so far away.'

'We must suggest it to him, but first we must both change. Look, you are dripping everywhere.'

'I apologise, my love. I'll return to my own rooms and change my raiment. Shall we go and see how Aunt Elizabeth and Amanda are progressing with the patterns and material? After that, it will be time to get ready for dinner. I hope you don't intend to put on that ridiculous ensemble again?'

'Absolutely not,' Sarah replied quickly. 'I cannot think what possessed me to do so last night. However, I shall change into a pretty gown, and you should do the same. Amanda has several of mine to choose from, so I'm sure she will change as well.'

Cressida was about to enter her own chamber when the sound of raised voices coming from the entrance hall alarmed her. If she was not very much mistaken, it was Papa shouting, and she couldn't remember ever hearing him so enraged.

8

Guy saw the ladies sloping off and decided to follow suit. 'Hadley, I need to speak to my man when he arrives, so I'm sorry but you will have to finish this enterprise by yourself.'

'Before you go, sir, I need to talk to you. I can't speak to my father, and I'm hoping you can advise me how to get out of this damned situation.'

'Go ahead. If you're thinking of touching me for a loan, don't. However, my advice, for what it's worth, is freely available.'

'I met up with some fellows at the local hostelry and got playing. I was suspicious when they let me win and tried to throw in my hand but they wouldn't let me. I'm convinced they were cheating, in it together, determined to fleece every penny I had. I was forced to put in avowals; God knows how much I owe those bastards. I was obliged to abandon my horse and escape through a window, as they threatened to hold me captive until someone arrived to pay what they said I owed them.'

'That explains why you were on foot yesterday. Do these villains know your whereabouts?'

'That's the thing, sir. I didn't give my real name, and nobody at the Hare and Hounds would reveal my identity.'

'Surely your horse will cover what you owe?'

Hadley stared morosely at his feet. 'The ostler there knows that the horse belongs to my father and will have hidden him away somewhere.'

'From what you tell me, Hadley, this is not your fault. Can you not explain it to the colonel and get him to deal with the matter?'

'Pa said if I got into a scrape again he would send me away. He won't give a jot for the fact that I was cheated, but insist that I shouldn't have been gambling in the first place. I don't want to go to India or America — I suffer most dreadfully from seasickness.'

Guy buried his face in his muffler in order to disguise his smile. Young Hadley might be two and twenty, but he was a long way from being an adult able to take care of himself. If he could settle this matter without involving Colonel Hadley and upsetting the household just before the festive season began, then he would do so.

'I take it you're worried these villains will follow you here and create unpleasantness.'

'It's only a matter of time, my lord. If the bribe is big enough, someone will give them the information they require.'

'Cheer up, my boy; I'll take care of this for you. I won't pay your debts, but I will get rid of the problem and hopefully keep news of this unfortunate incident from your father.'

The young man straightened, and his expression changed from despondent to happy in an instant. 'Thank you, sir. I shall be forever in your debt. I've no wish to build a snowman — shall we abandon our attempt and get into the warm?'

They were about to trudge through the snow towards the side door when four grinning youths dashed towards them. It would seem the ladies had sent reinforcements. Guy left Hadley to explain to the eager lads how he wished the snowman to look, and made his way through the snow to the stable yard so he would be there when his man arrived.

Tom slid from the back of his shaggy mount and touched his cap. 'There's good news and bad, my lord. Your missing luggage was safely at the Hare and Hounds, and I've managed to hire a cart and two farm horses to transport everything here. If the weather holds fine, they'll come tomorrow morning.'

'And the bad news?'

'The mail coach don't call there, and the nearest place to leave them letters is five miles away. I left them with the landlord, and he give me his word he would have them taken when the lanes are clear.'

'You did your best, and there's nothing more I can do. I shall need your assistance again for another matter, but it won't be until tomorrow, so get into dry clothes and get warm.' Guy dipped into an inside pocket in his riding coat and removed a silver sixpence. He tossed it to Tom, who caught it expertly in one mittened hand and, with a happy smile, touched his cap for a second time.

Hadley had gone in before him and left the side door open. The valet was waiting to remove Guy's wet outer garments, which he then handed to a footman. He waited whilst the man dried and polished his snow-encrusted boots. 'My luggage and valet should be arriving tomorrow. You have done an excellent job taking care of me; I shall make sure Grimshaw is aware of that.'

He would dearly like something to read and was confident he could find the library, which had been pointed out to him yesterday. He needed to cross the vaulted entrance hall and take the passageway opposite the one that led to the dining rooms.

When he was about to open the library door, he heard Colonel Hadley and young Hadley having a noisy dispute. His intervention would probably escalate matters, but in all conscience he couldn't stand aside.

He heard the colonel roar, 'Am I to understand, boy, that you have gambled away my favourite horse?'

'I'm trying to explain to you that your horse is perfectly safe — '

'Don't add falsehoods to your perfidy, boy. You're a disgrace to the name of Hadley, and I shall have you away from here as soon as may be. I'll have no more of your nonsense.'

Guy stepped forward at the same time as Cressida must have come from upstairs. He was about to speak when she shook her head vehemently. He took the hint and slid back into the shadows where he couldn't be seen, while she stepped forward and opened the door.

'Papa, kindly moderate your tone,' she said. 'You're not on the parade ground now, and we have guests who should not be obliged to hear you ranting at Richard like this.'

Good God, thought guy. This was like pouring oil on the fire — Colonel Hadley wouldn't take kindly to being taken to task like this by his daughter. But instead of further vitriol being spouted, the colonel stopped in mid-sentence, and his hectic colour began to fade.

'I'd forgotten we're not alone. You are right to tell me, my dear. I have a shocking temper.'

Guy couldn't prevent his snort of laughter and found himself the centre of attention. He stepped into view and smiled in what he hoped was a non-inflammatory way. 'I think, Colonel Hadley, that you might be said to be stating the obvious.'

'By God, sir, you have the right of it. Richard, I apologise for not listening to your explanation. I think we'd better remove ourselves to my study, where we can shout at each other without fear of upsetting the ladies.' Fortunately this was said without rancour, and the atmosphere became less tense.

Richard looked helplessly at Guy, who reluctantly felt obliged to offer to accompany them. He glanced at Cressida, and this time she nodded. Her radiant smile was more than enough to make up for whatever might be going to happen.

She beckoned him and he hurried over. 'Thank you,' she said. 'Papa will not lose his temper again if you're there. Don't raise your eyebrows at me, Bromley — I can assure you my father will have forgotten your vigorous exchange of words last night. I take it Richard has explained everything to you and is no doubt relying on you to get him out of this mess. I agree with Papa — it's high time my brother took responsibility for his actions, but I don't want him to be sent away.'

'Don't worry, sweetheart. Your brother won't be going anywhere. I give you my word on that.'

★　★　★

Cressida was unable to move for several moments after the three gentlemen had marched off. Not only had Bromley addressed her as *sweetheart*, but she had barely restrained herself from reaching out and touching his hand. He had also rashly promised to extricate her brother from his troubles and persuade the colonel to give Richard one more chance. They had decided to cordially dislike each other, so why were things changing between them so quickly?

She would dearly love to be a fly on the wall whilst this matter was discussed, but she had more urgent matters to think about. She must remove her damp and chilly garments before she caught a sore throat. Time enough to discover what plan Bromley had in mind when they met again for dinner.

The shutters were back and the curtains drawn in her apartment when she arrived. She glanced at the mantel clock and was shocked to see the hands pointing at a quarter past three. They kept country hours at the Abbey, and dinner would be served promptly at five o'clock, which meant there was little point in her changing into an afternoon gown and then changing again for the evening. Instead, after she'd removed her wet clothes she put on clean petticoats and covered these with a warm negligée. As she had no intention of wandering about outside her own domain, there was little likelihood of anybody being aware that she was incorrectly dressed.

'Polly, do I have something elegant but warm to wear this evening? Not an evening gown, but still smart enough to be worn for dinner.'

'I'll find you something perfect, miss. I know the very thing.' The girl nodded towards the door. 'Lady Bromley has found something she likes, so I know she'll be changing too.'

'I doubt that his lordship will don any of the items in his trunk, but I expect he'll put on a fresh shirt and stock. Lady Amanda has several of Sarah's gowns, so will be able to dress as well.'

A parcel of new books had arrived from Hatchards just before the weather worsened, and Cressida had discovered a delightful novel called *Pride & Prejudice*. She was enjoying it immensely and welcomed a quiet hour or so in which to immerse herself in the story.

'I'll take these wet clothes down to the laundry, miss, and collect the clean items,' Polly said. 'I'll be back in good time. Is there anything else you need?'

'No, run along. I'm content to sit and read in front of the fire.'

Despite the excellence of her novel, Cressida found it hard to settle, as she

144

was worried about what was going on downstairs with her brother. She was disturbed a while later by a sharp tap on the door and waited for Polly to answer it. Then she recalled that her maid had gone downstairs. She was so comfortably curled into the armchair that she had no wish to get up. She assumed that Richard had come at last to tell her what had transpired in the study, and so said, 'Come in; I've been waiting to see you this age.'

The door swung open, and to her horror Guy stepped in. 'Cressida, I'd no idea you were pining for me. I'm not sure whether to be flattered or alarmed at your interest.' Ignoring her immodest state of dress, he strolled in and sat on an upright chair at the far side of the room. Fortunately he had the good sense to leave the sitting room door open and not move his chair any closer.

'You cannot be in here,' she objected. 'Go away at once. I thought you were my brother. I've no more interest in you than I have in a stableboy, so don't sit there looking so pleased with yourself.'

His smile made her toes curl, and she wished now that she had put her feet on the floor and arranged her skirts more demurely. She was at a decided disadvantage, sitting like a child with her feet tucked underneath her.

He ignored her outburst as he had her ensemble, crossed his long legs at the ankle, and folded his arms across his chest. 'There is no need to be so snippy, Cressida. I come bearing good tidings which I thought appropriate, considering it's the season of goodwill to all men.'

It was impossible to remain cross when he was being so charming. 'Well done, Bromley; you have scored two points. Now it's my turn.' She pursed her lips and thought for a moment. 'The holly and the ivy must be collected tomorrow, which will bring joy to the world — well, to this household anyway.'

'Bravo! Shall we be serious for a moment? Richard explained to your father what had taken place, and that he had been gulled by cheats. However, it was the news that the colonel's precious gelding had not been handed over in payment of debts that restored the peace. The three of us are to go to the inn as soon as we can and confront these villains. I believe the colonel to be eagerly anticipating being able to use his military skills once more. Hopefully that will be the end of the matter, and the IOUs will be recovered and destroyed.'

'A far happier outcome than I anticipated, and I believe we have you to thank for it. Richard and my father cannot be in the same room for more than a quarter of an hour without being at daggers drawn.'

'Our brothers appear to have struck up a firm friendship, as have our sisters — and, dare I say it, our parents. We appear to be the only two still at outs with each other. Shall we call a truce and start again?'

Cressida couldn't help herself; she

wanted to refuse but heard herself agreeing. 'I give you my word I'll try not to be a shrew, if you'll promise not to be so curmudgeonly.'

His eyes narrowed, and for a moment she thought she'd overstepped and offended him, but then he smiled and nodded. 'I'll do my best to remain sunny and bright throughout the next two weeks.' He stood up and strolled to the door, pausing as he reached it. 'Permit me to say, Cressida my dear, that you're wearing a most fetching outfit. I don't believe I've ever seen a lady in her negligée before.'

She hurled her precious book with deadly accuracy and it hit him squarely in the chest. His stunned expression was quite comical, but he recovered his balance, and with terrifying slowness reached out and picked up the ruined item. 'That was uncalled for and unpardonably rude. If my sister did such a thing, I would put her over my knee and give her a sound spanking.'

The fact that she was inappropriately

dressed and her feet were bare no longer bothered Cressida. She almost threw herself from the chair, and instead of retreating she closed the gap between them. She met him icy stare for icy stare. 'My opinion of you will not change, Lord Bromley. You are arrogant, condescending and violent. I wish to have nothing more to do with a man who threatens physical violence to a woman or child. In future you will address me as Miss Hadley. Our temporary friendship — if you could call it that — is at an end.'

His eyes were so dark they seemed the colour of night, and she braced herself for a scathing retort. But he gave her a barely discernible nod and strode out of the room, leaving her with trembling knees and roiling stomach.

She stumbled back and collapsed onto the chair again. Only then did she realise she had accused him of being violent when it was she who had thrown a heavy book at him. What was wrong with her? She hadn't lost her temper since she was in leading strings, and certainly had never thrown an object at anyone with the intention to hurt.

★ ★ ★

Guy burst into his sitting room, sending his manservant scuttling back into the dressing room in shock. He had gone to see Cressida (she would never be Miss Hadley to him again, whatever he was obliged to call her) expecting to be received warmly. Indeed, that had been the case initially, but then everything had changed.

Cautiously he pushed aside his stock and pulled open his shirt front to examine the damage done by the book. There was already a purplish-black bruise forming, and it was damned painful when he breathed too deeply. Could the book have broken something? It was certainly thrown with sufficient venom and the intention to do damage.

Why had she reacted so violently?

150

His remark had been light-hearted, as had the rest of the conversation. He reviewed what he said and his fury drained away and was replaced by embarrassment. Although not meant to be offensive, his words could be taken to mean he considered Cressida of uncertain morals.

He wanted to pick up the coal scuttle and hurl it through the window but restrained himself. This was the second time he'd spoken thoughtlessly and deeply upset the young lady he was coming to regard as slightly more than an acquaintance.

He sunk onto the chaise longue and dropped his head into his hands. He was famous for his reserve, his calm demeanour and his impeccable manners, and yet in the space of one single day he had behaved like the veriest greenhorn.

What had he been thinking of when he'd all but threatened her with a beating? He'd never raised a hand to any of his family and never would. He'd had one or two bouts of fisticuffs at school and again at university, but these were fair fights between equals. The thought of hurting a member of the fairer sex or a child was unthinkable. He had no time for those gentlemen who thought of their wife and family as no different to their horses. Indeed, he was quite sure that some men he knew would more readily thrash their wife and children than lay a finger on their precious animal.

Jones coughed nervously from the safety of the bedchamber. 'The hot water has come from the kitchens, my lord, and I believe I have found a pair of breeches that will be acceptable until your own clothes arrive.'

'There's plenty of time,' Guy replied. 'It's another three quarters of an hour before dinner. There's something I must do before I change.'

9

Cressida scarcely noticed what Polly held out for her to step into. She sat with her eyes closed whilst her hair was being dressed and then walked out without a second glance. The thought of spending an evening in Lord Bromley's company was a daunting prospect.

She had behaved appallingly, and when he gave her the cut direct it would be no more than she deserved. The fact that they were no longer speaking to each other would be painfully obvious to everyone, and she prayed neither her siblings nor her father would decide to intervene on her behalf.

The long clock in the hall struck the hour, five o'clock, as Cressida made her way to the dining room. Usually everyone would be here by now, but she appeared to be the only person present at the moment. If she hid away at the far end of the room, she could avoid coming face to face with her adversary.

'Miss Hadley, I have a note for you,' Grimshaw spoke from behind her, causing her heart to skip unpleasantly. She turned and he held the silver salver out. She picked up the missive and turned it over. The serial pressed into the red blob of wax was unmistakable — it was the Bromley coat of arms.

She had no wish to read this in public, so slipped into a little-used antechamber. There was no fire, of course, and the room was horribly cold, but it would serve the purpose. With shaking fingers she broke the wax and opened the letter.

My dear Miss Hadley,
No doubt you are mystified as to why I should feel the need to write to you when I shall be seeing you very shortly.
I don't understand why we are

both behaving so out of character
— I am quite certain that you do
not make a habit of throwing objects
at people. I, for some inexplicable
reason, only have to open my mouth
in order to put both feet firmly in it.

I spoke without thinking and
should not have mentioned your
delightful ensemble, and certainly
should not have given you the
impression I thought you were not
behaving in a ladylike manner.
I apologise unreservedly and hope
you will forgive me.

I also want to make it perfectly
clear that I've never raised a hand to
my family and would never do so.
Like you, I think a man who abuses
his wife and children is despicable
and is no gentleman.

I would take it kindly if you
would continue to call me Bromley,
but I understand if you no longer
wish me to use your given name.

I am yours to command,
Bromley

His bold black scrawl almost jumped off the page at her. Her eyes filled as she reached the end of the note and saw how he'd finished. He might be a trifle proud, but he was a good man, and she had misjudged him. She had no handkerchief, as her reticule was in her bedchamber, and she could hardly wipe her eyes and dry her nose on her sleeve.

She had no option but to return to her apartment, as she could not appear in front of the others with tears on her cheeks and her nose dripping. She was chilled to the bone but scarcely heeded it. Bromley had forgiven her and was prepared to start again, and the thought of what this might lead to gave her a warm glow inside.

She sniffed inelegantly and carefully folded the letter so it could be concealed within her hand, as she had no wish to discuss its contents with anyone apart from the gentleman who wrote it. She dashed headlong from the room and almost collided with Bromley.

Although she tried to hide her face, he must have seen her tears, and he pushed a soft white cotton square into her hand. 'Here, sweetheart — dry your eyes and blow your nose. Why are you so overset? I didn't mean my letter to distress you.'

He was standing so close that she was aware of the heat pulsing from his body. She did as he suggested, but then was at a loss to know where to dispose of the soiled handkerchief. He gently removed it from her grip and it disappeared whence it came.

'Come, you're shivering; let us continue this conversation in front of the fire. The drawing room is still unoccupied, and we should have a few minutes in private before the others arrive.'

Instead of offering her his arm, he placed it around her waist and guided her across the hall. He didn't pause until they were standing in front of the welcome warmth of a roaring fire.

'I was overwhelmed by your letter

because I don't deserve your forgive-
ness,' Cressida explained. 'It's I who
must apologise, and I do so with all my
heart.' She raised her head, and of its
own volition her left hand moved to rest
lightly on the place where the book had
struck. 'Did I hurt you very much? My
book is quite beyond repair, and it's no
more than I deserve.'

His hands covered hers and his eyes
burned. What might have happened
next, Cressida would never know, as the
sound of voices outside the door meant
they were about to be joined by the rest
of the party. Guy released her instantly
and stepped away as she turned her
back on him and held her hands to the
fire.

The note she had secreted in her
right hand dropped to the carpet.
Before she could stoop to pick it up,
Guy reached past her and removed it.
He spoke so softly that she barely heard
his words. His breath on her neck made
her dizzy with excitement.

'I shall keep this safe for you and

return it when we are alone again, unless you wish me to burn it?'

'No, I should like to keep it.'

Richard strolled in with Amanda on his arm and Sarah close behind. 'There you are at last,' Cressida said. 'Grim-shaw has been prowling about with a face like thunder.'

'We apologise for our tardiness, Cressie, but we have been visiting with Harry,' her brother explained. 'He's insistent he will be carried to the sitting room tomorrow so that we can all spend time with him without breaching any rules of etiquette.'

'When I looked at his leg earlier today, the swelling had gone down considerably, and the bruising is not as bad as I feared. I think it will be safe enough for him to be lifted to his daybed tomorrow afternoon.' She turned to Guy. 'Perhaps you could organise this? I've no intention of giving him crutches for another day or two, but if he continues to improve then I see no reason why he shouldn't join us on Christmas Eve.'

Amanda looked around the room in surprise. 'Where is Mama? She left an age ago. I do hope she hasn't got lost.'

'Colonel Hadley is also absent,' Guy said with a frown. 'No doubt the two of them are closeted together as if society's rules don't apply to them.'

'Is that the way the wind blows?' Sarah said. 'How extraordinary. I would never have thought Aunt Elizabeth and Papa would get on together, as they are as different as chalk and cheese.'

A footman walked around with a tray of sherry wine but no one took it. Guy was glaring at the empty doorway, and Cressida was concerned he would be undiplomatic when their missing parents finally arrived.

The butler stomped in. 'Dinner is served, ladies and gentlemen. The master and Lady Bromley are already seated.'

This announcement produced the desired result, and all five of them made a dash for the double doors that led directly to the dining room. In order to avoid an unseemly muddle, Cressida hung back, as did Guy, allowing the others to rush through.

'What possessed my father to go to the dining room without coming in here first?' Cressida mused. 'We always gather in the drawing room, and he would be the first to complain if we did not.'

'Is it possible he did it deliberately in order to spend time alone with my mother?'

'Although I agree with Sarah that they seem an unlikely couple, I could not help but notice how animated my father is in Aunt Elizabeth's company.'

Much to her surprise, Guy chuckled. 'I love my mother dearly, but I'm the first to admit she's not an easy woman to live with. She flits from one thing to another and accompanies everything with a constant flow of trivial conversation. I need not tell you how much worse it is if she takes alcohol.'

'Good grief! Are you suggesting that this flirtation might become something permanent? I'm quite sure you are refining too much on the situation — your mother couldn't possibly wish to be married to a common person and live quietly away from the *ton*.'

Guy stopped dead and gripped her arm with such force that she winced. 'God's teeth! I've not even considered the possibility. My comments were meant as a friendly warning of what to expect over the next weeks, not that she might become your stepmama.'

There was no further opportunity to converse on this subject, as Grimshaw was now lurking in the doorway and would hear every word they said. They were the last to enter, and the guests had already arranged themselves. Amanda was sitting between Richard and Sarah, and the colonel and Aunt Elizabeth had taken the head of the table as they had done yesterday. This left the remaining two seats opposite Sarah and Richard.

Guy held out a chair for Cressida and then solemnly flicked open her napkin and draped it across her lap as if he were a footman. She nodded regally, and he smiled and took his place beside her.

'There you are at last! We had almost decided to begin dinner without you,' Aunt Elizabeth said. She gestured around the small party and beamed. 'I see we have all made an effort with our appearance tonight. I do so enjoy dining when everybody is dressed to impress.'

Cressida glanced around the assembled company and saw that this comment was correct. Apart from Bromley, everyone was looking very fine. Aunt Elizabeth's gown was old-fashioned but suited her to perfection, for she still had an excellent figure, and the gold brocade emphasised her tiny waist and rounded bosom. Although a widow and of middle years, she hadn't adopted the wearing of a turban or a lace cap.

163

'When will Harry be able to join us here?' Amanda asked as she helped herself from a dish of pike in lemon sauce.

'His leg is healing very well,' Cressida said. 'I've told him he may sit in his dressing robe on his daybed tomorrow afternoon. If he has no ill effects from that, then perhaps he could be carried from his apartment to spend the evening with us the day after.' She wasn't sure this was entirely wise, but the young man would become despondent if kept away from company for much longer.

'Why don't we spend the afternoon with him playing cards and other parlour games?' Sarah asked.

Amanda clapped her hands. 'I should like that very much. Harry is not a great reader and prefers to be busy with his friends, riding, driving his new high-perch phaeton, or other such gentlemanly pursuits. I should hate to think of him becoming miserable on his own.'

The matter settled, conversation moved on to the weather, and it was decided that they would go in search of Christmas greenery the next morning if it remained sunny and the snow had not returned. Aunt Elizabeth and Amanda became involved in a conversation about people who were unknown to the rest of the table. The gentlemen discussed the peace in France, the poverty and starvation caused by returning servicemen who were unable to find gainful employment, and other masculine subjects. But when both Cressida and Sarah offered pertinent remarks, these were received with respect and consideration by all three gentlemen — even Bromley seemed happy to include them. For all his toplofty ways, he appeared to share the same political views as the colonel, which meant they could talk on the same subjects without fear of further confrontation.

Tonight Cressida believed it would be in order to leave the three gentlemen to their port whilst she took the ladies into the drawing room. 'I have found several pieces of music that are suitable for this time of year. Would you like to choose what we should sing together when the gentlemen rejoin us?'

All in all, the evening passed pleasantly. They sang for an hour or so, and then the gentlemen sat down for a hand of piquet while Cressida joined the ladies some distance away so they could work out an itinerary for the next two weeks.

'Plans are already in hand for the New Year's ball, Aunt Elizabeth,' she said, 'and I think we should keep our new gowns to wear then. We're not expecting other company over the festive season itself — although I intend us to have a pantomime of some sort which we shall perform for the edification and delight of our staff on Boxing Day, which is, as you know, the first weekday after Christmas. Christmas Day is on a Saturday, so that will mean we have our pantomime on

Monday. This gives us eight days to write the piece, learn our lines and find suitable costumes. Sarah, I shall give you the task of writing our pantomime. I thought the fairy story of Cinderella might be a good theme.'

'That's something that Harry would be good at, so you must work with him on the script,' Amanda said with complete disregard for the problem of a single lady being closeted in the apartment of a single gentleman.

'Amanda and I will take care of the scenery and other items we might need,' Lady Bromley said. 'That trunk of clothes you sent down for me, my dear Cressida, has several items that would be ideal for costumes. I hope that Colonel Hadley will participate in this production. It wouldn't be as enjoyable without him.'

'I think that if Bromley agreed to do it, then he will not refuse,' Cressida said cheerfully, hoping this would indeed be the case.

The group reconvened when the tea

trolley was brought in; and whilst everyone was happily munching through a plate of sandwiches and cake as well as tea, Cressida broached the subject of their proposed pantomime.

Richard was enthusiastic. 'Good show! I always thought I should tread the boards for a living. I shall play the handsome Prince Charming, of course.'

Cressida smiled. 'I think that Bromley, you must play the part of the King; and Papa, you must be Cinderella's father. Perhaps, Aunt Elizabeth, you would consent to be the fairy godmother?'

Guy nodded. 'In which case,' he said, 'I think that Amanda, you must take the part of Cinderella; and Sarah and Cressida can play the ugly sisters.'

If he was waiting for her to protest at his suggestion, he was sadly disappointed. 'An excellent notion,' Cressida agreed. 'We must dispense with the wicked stepmother.'

'No, I shall do that as well,' Lady Bromley said. 'The fairy godmother is never in the same scene as the wicked stepmother, so it will be perfectly possible for me to have both parts.'

'Does Harry play the pianoforte?' Cressida asked.

'Strangely enough, he is quite proficient on the instrument. He can provide the music. I'm sure nobody will be any the wiser if he is unable to use the pedals.'

The evening drew to a close at around eleven o'clock, and Cressida could not remember having ever enjoyed herself so much. Papa had already spoken to Grimshaw about the proposed excursion into the woods to collect evergreens, and she was confident a suitable horse and cart and two or three willing outside men would be ready whenever the house party wished to go out.

She needed to check on her patient before she retired, so took the guest staircase. She was unsurprised to find that Bromley was already there, but uncertain whether his visit was to do with fraternal concern or because he wished to speak to her in private.

Harry was already asleep, and she had no intention of waking him so late. 'I was delighted and surprised that both you and my father are prepared to join in our pantomime,' she said quietly to Guy.

'Not half as surprised as I am. Unlike my siblings and mama, I've never taken part in such an enterprise before. Would I be correct in saying that neither has the colonel?'

'You would indeed. I think our staff will be talking about his performance for years to come, because I'm very sure it will never happen again.'

Guy dipped into his waistcoat pocket and held out the note he'd written to her. 'I cannot think why you wish to keep this, sweetheart, but as promised I've kept it safe for you.'

She was strangely reluctant to close the gap between them in order to take it from his outstretched hand. There was something dangerous about him tonight that she didn't think she was capable of dealing with. He was looking at her in a most peculiar way, and his gaze made her pulse skitter, while a strange heat was pooling in her nether regions.

He was waiting for her to move, and she was unable to resist his magnetism. Slowly she inched towards him until she was able to touch the paper held in his fist. No sooner had she done so than he moved and his arms closed around her waist, and she was pulled inexorably closer until every inch was touching his hard frame.

10

Guy's heart was pounding. Holding Cressida in his arms like this made him feel like a young man again; made him remember that life could be exciting, and not one tedious chore after another. She was the most desirable, adorable young lady he'd ever met. He'd never felt like this before — even his wife Charlotte had never made his pulse race.

He was about to tilt her head and cover her mouth with his when sanity returned. This was no experienced woman he had in his arms, but an innocent, and kissing her would be despicable unless he was prepared to marry her. This thought pushed its way through his passion to eventually register, and it was as if he'd been plunged into an icy bath. His desire wilted and he dropped his hands and moved swiftly to the door. 'I must beg your pardon yet again,' he said. 'I was taking shameful advantage of you. I bid you goodnight.'

Her stricken look pierced his heart, but he must remain firm in his resolve not to be entangled in parson's mousetrap. Lusting after a young woman was not the same as loving, and was no basis for a marriage. He tried to soften his rejection by bowing but knew he'd failed miserably. He dodged through the door and closed it behind him, expecting to hear the sound of a missile hitting the wood at any moment. Cressida's expression had already changed from shock to anger. She might be the most unsuitable bride he'd ever met, but she was certainly interesting company.

With more speed than dignity, he shot into his own chambers and leaned heavily against the sitting-room door just in case she decided to follow him. He pressed his ear against the panel but could hear nothing untoward. She must have made her way to her own apartment and was prepared to let the matter drop for the moment. God knew how she would greet him on the morrow, but hopefully a good night's sleep would calm her and they could greet each other with civility.

He'd told his manservant not to wait up for him, as he was perfectly capable of disrobing without assistance when needs be. He tossed his shirt and cravat onto the floor and dropped his borrowed breeches onto the heap of white cloth on the boards. He frowned, and then stepped across and picked up his discarded garments and placed them into the laundry basket.

It took him some time to fall asleep, as his thoughts were filled with the prospect of spending several weeks in close contact with a young woman he wanted to make love to. He'd never thought of himself as a passionate man; had been as happy without a mistress as with one. But now for the first time his senses were aflame, and he could think of nothing else but making her his own.

* * *

Cressida stared at the closed door and was tempted to rush after him and tell him exactly what she thought of him. How dare he entice her into his arms and then reject her so callously? She wasn't the beauty of the family — Sarah held that position — but she had had her share of successes. There was still one local gentleman who still hoped she would change her mind and accept his proposal.

What was it about Bromley that both enraged and attracted her? He was much older than her — he must be one and thirty at the very least; and although well-formed, he was hardly an Adonis. His younger brother was far better-looking and much closer to her in age. So why were her feelings toward Harry like those of a sibling, whilst his infuriating brother made her heart race?

There was no point in dwelling on

this now; she must get to her own rooms and retire. Her maid had gone to her bed long ago, but Cressida's gown lifted over her head without the need for fiddly buttons being undone at the back. She tossed a few lumps of coal on the fire in her bedchamber and then scrambled into bed.

By the light of the flickering flames she reviewed the extraordinary incident between herself and the earl. She could not deny, however much she wished to, that she was drawn to him in some inexplicable way. She disliked him, and found his overbearing manner and arrogance not to her taste; but whenever he was in the room she was aware of it.

After her initial anger had faded, she was glad he hadn't kissed her; for if he had done so, he would have been honour-bound to offer for her. That would have been an unmitigated disaster for all concerned. In future she would make sure she was never alone with him. He would be gone in two weeks and then she need never see him again. His invitation for the family to visit had been courtesy only — there was absolutely no need for her to go to Bromley Court in the summer.

* * *

The rattle of the curtains and the sound of the wooden shutters being pulled back roused Cressida from a deep slumber. Sleepily she sat up. 'Good morning, Polly. What sort of day is it?'

'No more snow, miss, but a bit grey. I've put out your warmest gown and flannel petticoats. It's going to be a mite chilly in the woods.'

'What time is it? I feel as if I overslept this morning.'

'The same time I always wake you, miss — seven o'clock. Is it true that there's going to be a pantomime on Boxing Day?'

News of this had somehow reached the servants' hall, which meant that no one could withdraw their agreement to participate. 'Indeed there is, Polly. We shall do it in the ballroom, as there's already a raised dais at one end where the musicians stand.'

'Ever so exciting! I've never seen a show of any sort, not even mummers at a village fair. In the three years since I came here there's not been any sort of celebrations, apart from our gifts on Boxing Day and time off to attend church and visit our families.'

Cressida finished her bowl of chocolate but ignored the sweet roll that had accompanied it. 'Things are different this year, as we have house guests and wish to give them a memorable time.' She threw back the covers and stepped out of bed, shivering as her bare feet touched the cold boards.

'I have found your divided skirt, miss — the one you had made especially so you could ride astride. Would you like to wear that today?'

'I'd quite forgotten I owned such a garment. Thank you, it will be ideal. I'll require a bath before luncheon, Polly.

Make sure the kitchen has plenty of hot water, as our visitors might also require one.' Although few people of her acquaintance bathed regularly, at the Abbey all the family took one without fail every month, and sometimes more often than that. Cressida loved to immerse herself in a lemon-scented bath, but didn't like to ask for gallons of hot water to be fetched up the winding servants' staircase more than twice a month. Maybe her father could be persuaded to install one of these new-fangled bathing rooms. After all, his pockets were deep, and he had nothing else to spend his money on.

★　★　★

When Cressida arrived at Harry's apartment, he was no longer in his nightshirt, but more or less dressed and already installed on the chaise longue in front of the fire.

'Good morning, Cressie,' he greeted her. 'As you can see, I've pre-empted your instructions. My temporary valet found me a pair of voluminous breeches from somewhere and so I was able to dress. I promise that I'll not move from here unless I need . . . well, you know what I mean.'

'How did you get here? I hope you didn't hop.'

'Not a bit of it. Bernard here fetched three other stout fellows and they carried me.' He moved the blanket from his legs so she could examine the break.

'No damage done,' she said, 'and I think you'll recover more speedily now that you can receive visitors. My sister's coming here after we have been on our excursion to collect greenery. We wish you to help write the pantomime and play the piano when we perform it. It wouldn't have been permissible for her to come whilst you were in bed.'

Harry grinned, and it made him look even younger than his two and twenty years. 'In which case, Miss Hadley, your reputation must now be in tatters.' He clutched his chest in a comical way. 'I must do the right thing. Will you do me the honour of accepting my hand in marriage?'

'My word, that was quick. Am I to offer my congratulations?' Bromley strolled in and winked at Cressida as he went past.

Getting into the spirit of the occasion, she clapped her hands and fluttered her eyelids. 'Oh my to think I am about to become a member of the aristocracy. Lord Harry, I should be delighted to accept your kind offer.'

Bromley looked stunned, and Harry's face drained of colour.

'However, I could never marry a man with a broken leg. Indeed, only the most perfect of specimens will ever gain my approval.'

'I say, that was capital fun. You had me worried for a moment, old thing.' Harry laughed but he still looked a trifle pale.

'Seriously, I can see why you might think that my being in your bedchamber has somehow compromised me

— but I can assure you that's not the case. I never attended you without at least two other people being in the room with us, so my reputation remains intact.' Cressida couldn't resist flicking a glance towards Guy, who looked suitably uncomfortable.

'I wish I could come with you this morning,' Harry said. 'I much prefer to be outside and not cooped up indoors. However, I'm resigned to the fact and shall make no further complaints if I'm to be involved in your festive play. When is Sarah intending to join me? We must get this opus written today or you won't be ready to perform it on Boxing Day.'

Cressida had been thinking whilst he was talking and came to a sudden decision. 'If we move all the furniture to the far end of this room, there's ample space for us to rehearse in here, which will remove the necessity of carrying you to the ballroom.'

'An excellent notion,' Guy said, 'but I think we must leave my brother to his own devices if we are to breakfast and be ready to go out by ten o'clock. The outside men and horse and cart must not be kept standing about.' He didn't wait for her agreement but waved cheerily to his brother and strode off. This left her with the option of running after him, which would be most undignified, or turning her back and stamping like a child. Neither option appealed, so she resumed her conversation with Harry until a suitable time had elapsed.

'I have all the information I require, Cressie, and will be able to get on with this play whilst you're all out enjoying yourselves in the snow.'

'I promise Sarah will join you after luncheon and you can work together. As soon as the pantomime is finished, we must all make a copy.'

'Do you wish it to be in rhyming couplets?'

'Whatever is easiest — as long as it's not too complicated; for I doubt that any of us can become word-perfect if you write too much for each character.

Remember, we're doing this for our staff, so references to any of them would go down well. Sarah can give you their names and idiosyncrasies when she comes later.'

Cressida had already given him a pile of paper and put a small table next to his daybed on which were placed an inkwell and several pens. All he needed now was something to lean on, but she would leave that to his valet, as she didn't wish to be any later than she already was for breakfast.

The breakfast parlour was buzzing with lively conversation when she arrived, and she was unsurprised that her father had broken the habit of a lifetime and joined them. Lady Bromley was talking to him about the panto-mime and he appeared engrossed. Sarah and Richard were in a lively debate about scenery with Amanda, which just left Guy for her to talk to.

He saw her hesitation and half-smiled. 'At last. If you had delayed much longer, we would have devoured everything.' He was on his feet before she could protest and picked up a large plate. 'If you would care to be seated, my dear, I shall collect whatever you wish to eat.'

Her appetite had inexplicably deserted her, but she could hardly tell him that. 'Eggs and ham for me, if you please, and a slice or two of fresh bread.'

There was already a selection of beverages on the table from which they helped themselves. He had abandoned his own breakfast in order to serve her, and with four others in the room to observe her actions, she could hardly sit on her own at the far end of the table. She took the seat adjacent to his but left an empty chair between them — hopefully this would indicate to him she had no wish to talk to him but would not be noticed by anybody else.

'Here you are,' he said. 'We all need to eat heartily if we're to brave the elements in half an hour.'

Immediately her father shook his head. 'Lady Bromley will not be accompanying you; it's far too cold. You young folks can gather what's necessary whilst we remain in the warm, applauding your efforts.'

'Five of us should be sufficient, Papa,' said Cressida, 'but I'll require everyone to help with the manufacturing of the garlands. I would have liked to have had the house decorated by the twenty-first, as that's the winter solstice. However, as you are no doubt aware, that date has gone.'

'I've got four men out searching for a suitable log to put in the fireplace in the Grand Hall,' he said. 'It must be big enough to burn throughout the twelve days.'

Sarah put down her cutlery. 'I seem to recall, Cressie, that there's a trunk filled with ribbons and trinkets that were used for decoration in our grandparents' time. Shall I send somebody to the attic to find it?'

'Please do that, my love. I can just remember the house in its festive finery — it must have been the year before

Grandmother passed away. Richard, you would have been seven years of age; you must have a better memory of this than I.'

'Why ask me, Cressie? The colonel's sitting right here — surely he is the person to ask.'

'I don't believe you were here that Christmas, were you, Papa? Were you not away somewhere with your regiment?'

Her father's brow creased. 'To be honest, my dear, I scarcely noticed such things. However, when I was a boy and came home for the holidays I do recall that the house always looked gay. I believe there were garlands of holly, ivy, and other such stuff along the mantelshelves. There were red, green and gold ribbons intertwined with the greenery and the Abbey looked quite different.'

Cressida and her siblings stared at him as if he had been speaking in tongues. For he had never before, to her knowledge, commented on anyone's appearance, let alone the fittings and fixtures of the house. Therefore, for him to describe the decorations so vividly was beyond belief. He was a man of few words, most of them to the point and frequently highly critical.

Cressida recovered her voice first. 'That's splendid. Papa, I now know exactly what to do. Although I've no expectation of you assisting with this task, I hope you will cast a knowledge-able eye over the results and tell me if they resemble what used to be done in the old days.'

'Get as many of the servants involved as you need, Cressida. I'm sure they will enjoy having a change of duties.'

'When I was a girl, we used to have wassailing on Twelfth Night,' Lady Bromley said. 'Do you think we could have the same this year, Colonel Hadley?'

He beamed and nodded. Indeed, Cressida believed that if she had asked him to bark like a dog, he would have agreed.

'This year we shall have whatever anybody requires to make this a Christmas to remember,' the colonel declared. 'I cannot think why we have not done this before, but in future we'll do it every year. I shall draw up an itinerary with Lady Bromley. Today is already planned, and tomorrow we shall all be involved with decorating this grand house. Bay trees and boughs must be fetched from the kitchen garden — and I shall demand that Grimshaw find as many beeswax candles as you need to complete your transformation, Cressida.'

There was a murmur of approval from all around the table, and even Guy seemed happy at the prospect of non-stop jollity and celebrations.

★ ★ ★

At precisely ten o'clock, Richard, Sarah, Amanda, Guy and Cressida were suitably dressed for the snow and ready to leave. They were accompanied by four men and a cart drawn by a sturdy horse that was warmly covered with a blanket against the elements. There were various tools in the cart with which to cut branches.

'Richard, I seem to remember there's a circle of holly trees on the east side of the wood,' Cressida said. 'Shall we head there first?'

One of the men, almost unrecognisable beneath his muffler and heavy outdoor coat, touched his cap. 'Miss Hadley, I sent one of the lads to have a look and he found exactly what you want. There's holly with plenty of berries, both fir and yew trees and ivy climbing everywhere.'

'In which case, we shall follow you.'

The horse and cart were about to plod off when Guy snatched her up and tossed her into the vehicle. Richard then did the same for Amanda, but Sarah scrambled up without assistance.

'You ladies might as well travel in style. It's far easier for us gentlemen to wade through the snow,' Guy said.

'That is very possibly the case, sir,' Cressida responded, 'but I would have preferred to climb in under my own volition and not be thrown in by you like a parcel.'

He laughed at her annoyance and dropped back to talk to Richard as if she didn't exist. If there was one thing she disliked above any other, it was being deliberately ignored.

'Have you noticed that there is a goodly amount of snow in this cart?' Cressida said to her companions. 'Even though we're sitting on sacks, it would be far more comfortable if we got rid of this nasty white stuff, don't you think?' She nodded at the two gentlemen walking along without a care in the world. The girls understood her intention immediately.

11

'Are you primed and ready to visit the village this afternoon, Hadley? According to my groom, the route is perfectly possible on horseback or with a farm cart.'

The young man shrugged. 'I'm not sure about this plan of action, Bromley. They were nasty coves and had more than one grimy henchman in tow. We could find ourselves in deep water.'

Guy slapped him on the back. 'There will be the three of us, plus some men with cudgels. I'll take my pistol, and your father will no doubt be armed to the teeth.'

A sudden movement from the cart a few yards ahead caught his attention. Before he had time to take evasive action, a large, hard snowball hit him squarely in the face. Caught off balance, he stumbled backwards and his boot sank into a pothole. The next thing he knew, he was flat on his back in the snow.

Richard shouted a challenge at the girls and then leaned down and offered his hand. 'Up you come, Bromley. We have a fight on our hands already.'

By the time he was upright and had shaken the worst of the snow from his clothes, the two of them were being bombarded by missiles. The young ladies had an unfair advantage, as their vehicle was carrying them out of range.

'I'll not be bested by a parcel of chits,' Guy grumbled. 'This is war, and it's one we must win if we wish to hold our heads up.' He scooped up a handful of snow, compacted it, and then hurled it at Cressida. His aim was true, and she disappeared from view for a few moments. Richard was obviously an expert at snowball fights and was scooping and throwing as if his life depended on it.

They were trotting forward, aiming, throwing and rearming as they went.

After a few frantic minutes, Guy realised there had been no recent missiles from the cart. They had run out of snow.

'Do you call it quits?' he called. 'Do you give in to our superior force, or must we annihilate you?'

The three girls had sensibly pulled up the tailgate of the cart and were now hiding behind it. 'We have run out of ammunition, as you very well know. If we can call a truce to allow us to rearm, we shall continue this battle.' This was Cressida's voice, but her words were applauded by her cohorts.

'What do you think, Hadley? Shall we give them quarter, or finish the job and claim the victory?'

His companion laughed. 'I think we're being outmanoeuvred. Whilst we've been debating the issue, our men have been piling new snow into the cart. Prepare to take evasive action, my friend, for a second more deadly attack is imminent.'

No sooner had he finished speaking

than a fusillade of snowballs arrived, knocking Guy's beaver to the ground and sending snow down his neck. Taking Richard's advice, he shot behind a tree and continued to throw from there until the cart was out of range.

'Is it my imagination, or has that horse increased its pace? I swear your men are ganging up on us.'

'They are indeed,' Richard replied. 'My sister Sarah is as thick as thieves with the outside men, and they would do anything for her. I can think of only one way to defeat them — we must get ahead and ambush the cart.'

Guy followed him in a headlong dash through the thickets and trees in order to accomplish this aim. They emerged after a few minutes in a clearing. 'Look — they'll arrive by that track over there, Bromley,' Richard breathed. 'This is obviously the place we're being led to.'

Guy looked around and immediately saw there were two big holly trees smothered in red berries, as well as other evergreens and a variety of fir trees. The cart would be there at any moment, so they had to get their ambush ready.

'I shall secrete myself behind that oak tree,' he said. 'You take the one on the other side of the path. Quickly, man — I can hear them coming.'

He was barely in place when the man leading the sturdy horse became visible in the gap. Guy already had a dozen snowballs made, and there was plenty more to be found on the branches that surrounded him. He paused, held his breath in anticipation, and then unleashed a flurry of snowballs on the unsuspecting trio laughing in the back of the cart. Richard did the same, and the victory was theirs.

'Pax! We give in. Please stop; we are fairly vanquished,' Cressida yelled.

Sarah and Amanda joined in with cries of surrender and the impromptu fight was over. Guy bounded over to the cart and stopped in astonishment.

'Hell's teeth! Did we do this? You are scarcely recognisable as smart young ladies out for a jaunt.' He unhooked the tailgate and reached in to remove his sister. He thought it prudent to allow Cressida to scramble out on her own, as she appeared to have taken the brunt of their ferocious counter-attack.

The outside men who'd accompanied the party on this excursion looked away whilst the girls shook out their skirts and brushed each other down. 'I swear I've snow inside my gown as well is in my boots,' Amanda complained bitterly. 'I'll be a solid block of ice before we return.'

Richard grabbed her hand and pulled her across the clearing until they were beneath a holly tree. 'Here — we shall pick together, and by doing so you will get warm. This is a splendid tree! I've never seen so many berries.'

Sarah wandered off with two of the men and was soon busy stripping a tree trunk of long fronds of ivy. Cressida pointed to the naked branches of a tree a little distance from the clearing. 'There's mistletoe halfway up that tree over there. I should dearly like to have a kissing-bough in the centre of the ballroom. I know the custom's frowned upon, but I'm sure our staff would appreciate the effort that goes into making one.'

Guy viewed the tree with disfavour. 'Are you suggesting that I climb up and get it for you? Surely as the winner of the snow fight, it is for me to decide the forfeit?'

'I wasn't aware that there were forfeits involved, sir. And I had no intention of asking you to climb a tree. Good heavens, it would be far beneath your dignity to exert yourself in such a way.' Her teasing smile took the sting from her words.

'I find it difficult to admit, sweet-heart, but I've never had so much fun in my life as I've had since arriving uninvited and unannounced at your home.'

This comment pleased her, and her radiant smile sent a strange sensation from the top of his snow-covered head to the bottom of his frozen feet. He forgot about the mistletoe and turned his attention to snapping off lengths of fir and yew and dropping them behind him in the snow. When he had accumulated sufficient to make it worthwhile trekking over to the cart, he gathered up the pile and carried it across the clearing. He was pleased to see that the vehicle was almost half-full of a variety of evergreens, and his contribution left only a quarter to fill.

As he returned to the yew tree, he heard his sister scream.

★　★　★

Cressida stared up at the mistletoe. She was determined to have it, but thought the branches too flimsy for one of the gentlemen to attempt to climb. She had no option but to climb up herself. As she'd had the foresight to put on her divided skirt, she could do so without fear of exposing an indelicate amount of leg or run the risk of becoming entangled in flapping material.

If any of the gentlemen became aware of her intent, they would stop her. She glanced around the clearing and saw that everyone was busy about their tasks and paying her no heed. She forced her way into the thicket that surrounded the tree in which the mistletoe hung tantalisingly out of reach. There were several smaller branches, and these would be ideal to assist her in her climb. The distance was no more than three yards, so even if she did have the misfortune to slip, she was unlikely to hurt herself.

It was some years since she had shinned up a tree, but the skill soon returned to her; and despite the fact that the bark was slippery, she was able to reach the branch with comparative ease. Her concentration was entirely on the task and she had quite forgotten there were others in the clearing.

Just as she was reaching out to snatch the final bunch of mistletoe, Amanda screamed. The sudden sound so startled Cressida that she lost her grip. She was going to fall — but in desperation she clung onto the mistletoe and took it with her. Her landing knocked the breath from her lungs, and she was left gasping for air like a fish out of water.

Guy landed on his knees beside her, and she expected to receive his support and concern. What she got was another thing entirely.

'You stupid girl! What the hell were you thinking of? You could have been killed.' With brisk efficiency, he ran his hands from her shoulders to her ankles before sitting back, a grim expression on his face. 'You've broken nothing. When you have recovered your breath, you will be able to get up without my assistance.'

Being unable to speak was a distinct handicap when you wished to respond in kind. Then Richard and Sarah were next to her, and they smothered her with affection and gently helped her to her feet. Her first concern was for the mistletoe that had caused the problem. She saw it adjacent to the place she had fallen and was delighted to see it had escaped undamaged.

'Sarah, stop fussing — I'm perfectly well. However, I'm a bit stiff, so would you be kind enough to collect the mistletoe I went up the tree to pick?'

'Good grief!' Richard exclaimed. 'You risked your neck for a bunch of that ridiculous plant? I'm surprised at you, Cressie. I thought you the sensible one in the family.' He scowled at her and stomped off, leaving her alone with her sister.

'Are you going to castigate me too? I wouldn't have fallen if someone hadn't screamed — was it you?'

'No, I'm not going to scold you,' her sister said.

'I'm so sorry, but it was me who screamed,' Amanda confessed. 'I saw you halfway up that tree and panicked. This is all my fault. Now Bromley is enraged and the whole day ruined.' She had been standing beside Sarah unnoticed up until that point. The girl gulped and tears slithered down her cheeks.

'Please, don't cry,' Cressida said. 'I came to no harm and I've achieved my aim. If Bromley's cross, then that's his concern, but there's no need for any of us to think about the incident for another moment.' She put her arm around Amanda's shaking shoulders, and Sarah found a handkerchief from somewhere about her person and handed it over.

Someone cleared their throat loudly behind them and Cressida looked round. One of the outside men was standing there, cap in hand. 'I reckon we've got more than enough to decorate the whole place, miss, and the gentlemen have left. I'm afraid there's no room on the cart for you on the return journey.'

'Thank you. A job well done, and much appreciated. We're happy to walk back; it's less than half a mile. Come along, ladies — the sooner we set off, the sooner we shall be back and in the warm. I for one am going to take a hot bath and change into something more appealing before we gather for the midday repast.'

Amanda soon stopped sniffling and was chattering away about nothing very much by the time they reached home. Although Cressida had insisted she was perfectly fine, by the end of this short walk she was aware that she'd hurt her arm, as every step she took sent shafts of pain along the injured limb. Not wishing to alarm either of her companions, she carefully tucked it between two buttons on her cloak, and this was giving it some support. She prayed she'd done no more than sprain it, as she could hardly set her own arm, and she had no faith whatsoever in the local physician.

Sarah and Amanda dashed off as soon as they were through the door, leaving Cressida to make her own way. The closeness between the two was surprising, as Sarah had no time for frivolity and preferred to be outside with her horses, and Amanda thought of nothing but fashion and the latest gossip from London.

Cressida shook her head at the maid who was waiting to take her outdoor garments. 'There's no need; Polly will help me when I get to my room.'

The magnificent staircase had never looked so imposing or so difficult to ascend. Her legs were leaden and her head ached unpleasantly, which added to the pain in her injured arm and was making it difficult for her to find the energy to climb the stairs. If she made the attempt unaided, she risked, a far more serious injury, and that would be foolish. She must do something she never usually did: she must ask for assistance.

Somehow she stumbled her way into a small chamber that was for the use of unexpected callers. There was a bell-strap next to the door and she tugged it fiercely. With some difficulty, she found her way to an upright wooden chair and sank gratefully into it.

A footman answered her summons almost immediately. 'Would you be so kind as to fetch Mr Hadley?' she said. She closed her eyes and bit her lip, hoping she could remain in control of her spinning head long enough to reach her apartment.

The door opened and someone rushed in. However, it wasn't Richard's voice who spoke to her, but Guy's. 'Foolish child — you should have said you were unwell. I'm a brute to have shouted at you and then abandoned you. Where are you injured?'

His unexpected kindness was her undoing, and she couldn't stop her eyes overflowing. 'My arm is injured, my head hurts, and I feel most peculiar.'

'Can you put your sound arm around my neck?'

She nodded and sniffed, wishing he would offer her his handkerchief. 'My right arm is damaged, though my left is fine.'

He put one arm under her thighs and the other under her arms; then she was hoisted unceremoniously into the air. She grabbed his collar in order to steady herself. 'Around my neck, sweetheart; you're strangling me.'

This was a new experience for her, as she'd never been carried anywhere before. For some reason she felt safe in Guy's arms and relaxed, resting her damp cheek against his shoulder with a sigh.

'I know you expected your brother to come to your aid, but the three of them have already gone to their rooms. I was about to do the same when the footman arrived in search of Hadley.'

'Actually, you're the better choice, as I doubt Richard is strong enough to carry me on his own.'

Guy kicked open her sitting-room door and strode in as if he belonged there. He didn't stop, but marched across and straight into her bedchamber. Polly and the chambermaid were absent, which was unusual.

'Please put me down on the bed, Bromley,' Cressida said. 'And before you leave, would you be so kind as to pull the strap? My abigail must be overseeing the hot water for my bath.' Her cheeks flooded with unpleasant heat. How could she have been so indelicate as to mention she was going to take a bath?

Guy put her down and rang the bell, but didn't retreat as she'd expected. Instead he sat beside her and reached out to unbutton her cloak. 'No, little one, allow me to play the part of your lady's maid. This wet cloak must come off or you will catch a congestion of the lungs.'

She felt too unwell to protest and raised and lowered her arms as requested. He gently examined her injured arm. 'Although I'm no expert, Cressida, I believe this is merely bruised. However, I'm more concerned about your lethargy and the large lump on the back of your head.'

His voice appeared to be coming from a great distance away, and she was having difficulty seeing him. Then everything went black.

12

Guy caught Cressida as she lapsed into unconsciousness and carefully laid her back against the pillows. Where the devil was her maid? He'd rung some time ago.

Polly appeared from the dressing room and looked horrified to see him standing next to the bed. 'My lord, you shouldn't be in here.' Then she saw her mistress stretched out, as white as a sheet, and ran forward. 'Whatever next? What's wrong with Miss Hadley?'

Guy gave her a quick explanation of what had transpired but didn't apologise for being where he was. Servants were there to do as they were bid; there was no necessity to explain one's actions to them at any time. 'You will need to fetch warming pans and hot bricks — she's far too cold. Also, her right arm will need strapping up. I've examined it and am certain it's not broken.'

The girl curtsied and gestured to another maid, who was hiding behind the door. 'Quickly, Annie — we must get Miss Hadley warm and dry.'

This was Guy's cue to depart. 'I intend to send someone for the doctor,' he said. 'I'm sure somebody could get through today.'

'I beg your pardon, my lord, but we don't have Doctor Wilkins here. Miss Sarah is almost as skilled in such things as Miss Hadley, so I'll have her fetched immediately.'

'Then who the devil do you have when neither of the young ladies can solve the problem?'

'There's a new doctor in Huxley, but that's half an hour from here when the weather's good. We can't fetch him at the moment.' Polly stared pointedly at the door.

Guy was *de trop*, so despite his unease about this unorthodox approach to illness, he had no option but to retire. 'I shall remain in the sitting room until Miss Sarah has examined her sister.'

The door was closed firmly behind him and he went to stare morosely out of the window. What should have been a scene of enchantment now seemed like the work of the devil. His luggage and personal servants had yet to appear, and now they could not send for a competent physician to take care of Cressida.

Colonel Hadley had yet to be informed that his daughter had taken a tumble from a tree, so Guy decided he'd better go down and give him the bad news. Miss Sarah flew past but failed to acknowledge him. He was unused to being ignored and was finding it a salutary lesson.

On enquiry, he discovered that the colonel was still closeted with Lady Bromley in the small drawing room. No footman led the way or opened the door and announced Guy's arrival. This was another irksome detail of his stay here; he was accustomed to being shown the deference and respect his position merited.

He knocked on the door and was invited to enter. His mama was sitting on one side of an inlaid mahogany table and the colonel was seated opposite her. Neither of them got up at his entrance, although both looked up and smiled. Well, his mother smiled, and the colonel merely looked less disagreeable than usual.

'Colonel Hadley, I've come to tell you Miss Hadley fell from a tree whilst picking mistletoe. Although at first we all thought she was unharmed, she has badly sprained her right arm, and I believe might have a slight concussion. She is presently unconscious, and her maids and sister are taking care of her.'

His mother looked more concerned than the colonel. 'How dreadful!' she exclaimed. 'I shall go to her at once, for I'm sure I can be of some comfort to the girls at this worrying time.'

'No, my dear Lady Bromley — I'm sure my daughter will be perfectly fine,' the colonel interceded. 'Sarah will let us know if there's anything we need to do.' He glared at Guy as if it was his responsibility that his daughter was injured. 'Why was Cressida up a tree? Hardly a ladylike occupation. One of you gentlemen should have climbed to fetch the mistletoe.'

Guy half-bowed. 'I agree, sir, but Miss Hadley took matters into her own hands before any of us were aware of her intention. As she was able to walk home unaided before she suffered a collapse, I'm sanguine that she has suffered no serious hurt.'

'I shall see you at luncheon, Bromley, and will show you what the colonel and I have been planning for us to do on each of the twelve days of Christmas. I cannot tell you what fun I've been having since I got here. I must insist that in future Bromley Court celebrates in the old-fashioned way.'

Guy smiled but made no comment,

and then left them to their scribbling. He glanced at his pocketwatch and saw there was still an hour to go before luncheon would be served. There was ample time to visit his brother and bring him up to date with the events of the morning.

Nobody seemed at all concerned about Cressida's collapse. Was he the only one who found the situation less than ideal? Did he have a guilty conscience because he'd spoken so harshly to her and not offered her any assistance after her tumble from the tree? He closed his eyes and saw again that dreadful moment when Amanda had screamed. Cressida had lost her grip and fallen to the ground with a sickening thump. His heart had all but stopped. For a second he'd been paralysed by a fear that she had perished. When she started to gasp for breath, his unsympathetic reaction had been because of his relief.

The door to Cressida's sitting room was ajar, so he walked in just as Sarah entered from the bedroom. 'How is she?' he asked.

'A lot better, thank you, sir. I think it was shock at what might have happened that caused her collapse. Despite the nasty lump on the back of her head, I don't believe she is concussed, as she has no nausea or disturbed vision. Her arm will be better in no time if she agrees to keep it in a sling for a day or two.'

Things suddenly seemed a lot brighter. 'I'm delighted to hear you say so. I've informed our parents and was on the way to see my brother.'

'Richard is already there, and the three of us are writing the script for the pantomime. At the rate we're progressing, we shall be finished by three o'clock this afternoon, and then we must all gather and start copying.'

'I'll take it upon myself to copy for both myself and Cressida. Somehow I doubt that either the colonel or my mother will come here to do it.'

'With the five of us, we shall soon

have all the copies we need. I shall do one for my papa, Amanda is doing one for Aunt Elizabeth, and you are doing the extra one for my sister. I think we shall be able to start rehearsing tomorrow when Cressie is back on her feet.'

Cressida overheard this conversation and was touched that Guy had come to enquire after her health, and even more so that he'd offered to be her scribe. 'Polly, I'm going to sleep for an hour or so, and then I would like to take my bath. It's fortunate the water had not already been fetched up for me.'

'Miss Sarah wants you to stay in bed today,' Polly said. 'You took a nasty fall, and it's better to be safe than sorry.'

'I shall be perfectly well after a rest. Please wake me with a tray — hopefully there will be something left in the kitchen that I can have.'

Polly left, tutting and mumbling under her breath, and Cressida smiled. She rather liked the fact that her personal maid fussed over her, for it was certain nobody else did. Her arm ached a little, as did her head, but apart from that she felt remarkably well.

She fell asleep thinking about the forthcoming rehearsal for the pantomime, and was awoken by the welcome rattle of crockery on a tray and the appetising smell of leek and potato soup. After she had eaten and taken her bath, she dressed with more care than usual.

'My head is too sore for my hair to be put up or plaited, Polly. Could you restrain it in a ribbon?' Once this had been achieved, she tilted her head and stared critically at her reflection. 'I'm not sure appearing with my hair down is quite proper, but needs must, and we don't stand on ceremony in this house.'

With her right arm safely in a sling and her hair gathered loosely at the nape of her neck, Cressida set off for the apartment downstairs, where she hoped she would find the rest of the company preparing to rehearse the pantomime. From the noise coming from within Harry's sitting room, everyone was ahead of her.

She pushed open the door and stood for a moment, surveying the group. Richard and Amanda were head to head on the window seat reciting their lines, while her father and Aunt Elizabeth were standing by the fire doing something similar. Harry was deep in conversation with his brother; Cressida was struck by the similarity of the two despite their difference in colouring and stature.

Bromley looked up, and his smile made her clutch the door frame for support. 'At last! We did not wish to start until you arrived. I have your script here.' He was at her side in two long strides and offered his arm. 'Are you sure you're quite well enough to be here?'

'I'm sorry to have kept you waiting. And yes, I'm perfectly well, thank you for your enquiry.' She made what she hoped was a simpering expression. 'Are you suggesting, my lord, that I am not looking my best?'

He chuckled and took her left hand and put it on his arm. 'Fishing for compliments, my dear?' He turned his face away from the others and spoke softly. 'You look *ravisante*, sweetheart. You should wear your hair down all the time. It is magnificent.'

She could think of nothing to say in response to his compliments, so nodded and smiled, but kept her eyes firmly to the front. This was the first time the entire house party had been gathered together in one room, and she could not help but notice how people had paired off. It was hardly credible that romance was in the air for all four couples, but she was certain that to an outside observer it would seem that that was the case.

Harry had appointed himself director of the pantomime and called everybody to order. 'Apart from Cressie, everyone has had ample time to read their script, so we must start rehearsing.'

The remainder of the afternoon flew

past with hilarity and fun. To Cressida's astonishment, even her father got into the spirit, and strode about the space as Cinderella's unfortunate papa as if he was a real theatrical. Lady Bromley played both her parts to perfection.

When it was time to call a halt, they agreed it had been a most enjoyable afternoon. 'The script is funny, and writing it in rhyme will make it so much easier to learn,' Cressida told the assembled company.

Only Harry was quiet, and Sarah looked at him anxiously. 'It seems such a shame you will be excluded from the evening's entertainment,' she said. 'I suggest that we come here after dinner so we can play cards, charades or other silly games.'

This suggestion was received enthusiastically by the younger members of the party, but the colonel and Lady Bromley said they would prefer to remain in the drawing room. Bromley had been silent on the subject. Cressida was about to depart when a strange man stepped through from the bedchamber.

Harry exclaimed in pleasure. 'Bertie, you are here at last! That must mean that our luggage has finally arrived.'

The colonel looked equally pleased. 'In which case, ladies and gentlemen, we shall dress for dinner tonight. Cressida, do you think that Lord Harry could be carried along so he can join us?'

She was about to refuse, but he looked so eager she had not the heart. 'Very well, as long as you give me your word not to attempt to move once you are in place.'

Richard slapped the table with an open palm, causing every person to turn in surprise. 'Cressie, I'm certain there's an old bathchair lurking in this apartment somewhere. We can trundle Harry around in that if we can locate it.'

The older couple wandered off, presumably to begin their preparations for the evening; and Amanda, Sarah and Richard rushed off in search of the missing bathchair, leaving Guy alone with Cressida at the far end of the room. Harry was busy writing annotations on the scripts and taking no notice of either of them.

'In all the excitement of your accident — ' Guy began.

'I should hardly call falling from a tree exciting.'

'If you would allow me to finish, Miss Hadley, I was about to say your brother, the colonel and myself failed to visit the village and recover the avowals from those miscreants.'

His stern look made her laugh, but really there was nothing amusing about his comment. 'I suppose that as your luggage was able to get through to us, then those men, whoever they are, will now be able to do so as well.'

'I fear that you're correct. However, I think they will not be anticipating the sort of reception they will receive. After all, now that your father is cognisant of the circumstances, they will not be able to cause the mayhem they might have anticipated.'

'What do you think will happen when they eventually arrive demanding money with menaces?'

He shrugged as if indifferent. 'I expect one or other of us will remove the IOUs from their possession and then they will be sent about their business.'

He said this with such casual assurance that Cressida accepted his words without demur. He looked at her, and she thought he was about to say something interesting, when they were interrupted by the arrival of the three searchers triumphantly pushing a three-wheeled basketwork vehicle that her grandfather had used in his dotage.

Bromley examined it and pronounced it safe for use, and then the group departed to change for dinner.

Polly greeted Cressida with enthusiasm. 'Well I never did, miss. Such excitement! Now all the trunks have arrived. Lady Amanda's and Lady

Bromley's dressers are both very hoity-toity with Mrs Miller and are demanding this and that.'

'I'm sure things will settle down in a day or two. Mrs Miller will speak to me if there's anything I need to do. Now, what do you suggest I wear tonight? I cannot put my hair up, and I'm not sure that either of my evening gowns would be suitable with my hair loose like this.'

'I've thought of a way I can dress your hair so that it won't pull on your scalp. I can gather it into a loose chignon on the nape of your neck so you can wear either of the gowns and still look smart.'

At exactly five o'clock Cressida left her chamber and headed for the drawing room. Tonight the sound of voices meant that others had arrived before her. She was glad her demi-train had a loop of material attached to it so she could hold it from under her feet. With only one functioning arm, it would have been all but impossible to do this if she hadn't been able to slip the loop over her wrist.

Polly had found a square of material left over when the gown was made, and this now served as a sling. Confident she looked her best, she made her way towards the open doors, unaware she was being observed.

★   ★   ★

Guy spent longer over dressing than he was accustomed to. He had a feeling that everyone would make an extra effort tonight, and he had no wish to be found wanting. He told his man not to wait up, but to spend the evening in the servants' hall familiarising himself with the way the house was run.

As he reached the passageway that led to the central hall he saw Hadley, Sarah and Amanda arriving with Harry in the antiquated bathchair. He paused to allow them to enter before him, struck by what a handsome quartet they were. Indeed, he was surrounded by the most attractive company, and was a fair way to enjoying himself.

He was halfway across the chequered floor when a slight sound in the gallery above alerted him to the arrival of the young lady he was beginning to think of as someone rather special. Moving smoothly into the shadows, he turned to watch her descend.

His eyes widened in appreciation. How could he ever have thought of her as plain? She was a diamond of the first water, an incomparable, and she put all the rest in the shade. Her shiny tresses had been carefully arranged at the base of her neck and framed her oval face. Her golden evening gown was covered with a shimmering fabric that made her look ethereal. Her creamy bosom curved from the close-fitting bodice. Captivated, he allowed her to sweep past before stepping out of hiding.

'Good evening, Cressida. Allow me to say that you look quite beautiful tonight. That gown is exquisite and suits you perfectly. I cannot imagine there's a more attractive house party anywhere in the county.'

She stopped and turned to stare at him. 'Thank you, Bromley. And might I be permitted to return the compliment? Black and white suits you very well.'

He offered his arm and she placed her left hand on it. He walked in to join the others, feeling as proud as the king he was to play in their pantomime.

13

The next morning Cressida was up at dawn, eager to begin assembling the garlands and decorations that would make the house look festive. Her maid had volunteered to help and so was there to assist.

'I shall need something warm, Polly, as we shall be working in the flower room and that has no heating. We will also need gloves.' She hesitated, knowing she should not ask her abigail to gossip, but Cressida was eager to know anything that had been gleaned about their guests from the Bromley personal staff. The outdoor men hadn't had anything of interest to pass on about their employers. 'Did the Bromley staff join you in the servants' hall last night?'

'They did, miss. Lady Bromley's dresser thinks herself above the rest of us, but the other girl and the two valets were very sociable. They were full of the change they'd found in their masters and mistresses — I reckon Bromley Court has been a right old miserable place since Lord Bromley's wife died two years ago.'

Cressida jerked forward, pulling her hair painfully across the lump in the back of her head. Bromley was a widower — that explained his reserve. Had this been a love match or an arranged marriage? She would ask Sarah to bring the subject up with Amanda, for she could hardly ask Bromley for this information.

'There,' said Polly. 'That lace cap looks very pretty on you, miss, and it holds your hair nice and tidy.'

'We shall go down the back staircase together — I don't believe I've used it since I was a girl. It leads directly to the flower room, so it makes sense to go that way.'

'Are you putting on the sling this morning?'

Cressida flexed her wrist and shook

her head. 'No, I can use this arm perfectly well. I can hardly make garlands and suchlike with only one hand in use.'

With Polly walking in front carrying a candle, she followed behind, making sure she didn't step on the hem of her gown. She had forgotten how narrow and twisting the servants' staircase was. The sooner she could persuade her father to install bathing rooms upstairs, the better. Then only the hot water would have to be carried to the bedchambers, as the dirty water removed itself through the bottom of the bath.

When she walked into the freezing flower room, she stopped in surprise. There was not an inch of space that wasn't covered with heaps of holly, ivy, fir, yew, and in solitary splendour, the bunches of mistletoe she'd suffered to obtain. 'I'd no idea we'd collected so much. How kind of someone to arrange it so carefully, as this will make it much easier to construct the garlands.'

She walked through into the room that contained the vases and other items needed when arranging flowers for the house. 'Excellent. I see we have several baskets of ribbons, another of fir cones, and there are at least a dozen bay trees in pots that will look absolutely splendid once they're decked out in ribbon.'

This room was much warmer than the other, and it was here she decided to work. She and Polly had been busy for half an hour when Sarah and Amanda burst in.

'Good morning, Cressie!' her sister said. 'I can't believe we're down here working when it's scarcely light outside.'

'Thank you for coming to help. I shouldn't go into the other room and see just how much greenery there is to work with, for I fear it will send you rushing back to your apartments.'

Sarah looked in the flower room and nodded. 'The four of us will soon get this done, and if the gentlemen deign to join us later so much the better.'

They worked industriously until a parlourmaid popped in to tell them that breakfast was now being laid out. 'I'm absolutely starving,' Sarah said. 'I can't remember when I've been so hungry.'

Cressida surveyed what they'd done so far. 'We've accomplished far more than I could ever have imagined in the time. The garlands for the hall are ready to go up and the kissing bough is ready to be hung in the ballroom, and the decorated bay trees can be taken to the drawing room.' She turned to her maid, who was still busy weaving ivy through a wreath of holly. 'You must go and break your fast, Polly. You've done more than enough for one morning.'

'It makes a change from mending and ironing, miss. Do you wish me to come back here after I've eaten?'

'No, we'll manage. Thank you for your assistance.'

The three of them washed their hands in the icy water they discovered in a pitcher and then checked each other for stray pieces of ivy or other debris. Once satisfied they were all looking tidy, they hurried to the breakfast parlour.

Not only was Bromley and his mama there, but also his brother in his bathchair. Only the colonel was absent from the table. The three of them fell on the chafing dishes as if deprived of food for months, not allowing either of the gentlemen to get up and offer to serve them.

'We need your assistance, gentlemen,' Cressida said. 'There are garlands ready to be hung about the place, and that is a job for you.'

Guy raised an eyebrow in an irritating way. 'Don't you have footmen to do that sort of thing?'

'We do, of course, but they have more than enough to do without adding to their burden. Anyway, the rule is quite clear. Those who picked are obligated to be involved with the decorating of the house; therefore,

Bromley, you cannot weasel out of it so easily.'

'I'm sure that the colonel, Hadley and I would be absolutely delighted to scramble about putting up your garlands. However, we have more urgent business in the village to attend to this morning.'

Although this was said with a smile, Cressida detected something worrying behind his bland demeanour. She looked across at her brother but he refused to meet her eye. Sarah had heard Bromley's remark and spoke softly to her sister as they sat down together at the far end of the table from the gentlemen.

'Richard told me yesterday that they're going to confront the men who imprisoned him. Do you think that's wise?'

'Bromley says they will be well prepared, and with Papa in charge I'm certain it will be run like a military operation. Anyway, Sarah, they must recover the horse, which is still languishing in the stables at the inn.'

She joined the gentlemen at the table with her piled plate and there was no further opportunity to discuss this matter. Despite her worries about the forthcoming venture Cressida devoured her breakfast with enthusiasm.

They were on their third cup of coffee when a footman came in with a whispered message for Richard. Immediately he and Bromley put down their cutlery and stood up. Cressida looked at Guy, and he nodded and smiled in what he hoped was a reassuring manner. He hoped they would all return unscathed from this enterprise.

They found Colonel Hadley striding up and down the hall impatiently. 'The horses are waiting, gentlemen,' he said. 'We must leave immediately if we wish to accomplish this mission and be back in time for this afternoon's rehearsal.'

By the time he and Richard were suitably dressed, the butler had the door open and he had no option but to exit, despite his misgivings about this venture. He wasn't sure whether the colonel's reference to the pantomime or his appearance surprised him most. The man had donned his military regalia and was armed to the teeth. A nondescript gentleman of middle years, dressed soberly in a dark riding coat with only one cape, stepped forward and bowed.

'My lord, there are two pistols stashed behind your saddle; both are primed and ready to fire. You will find spare powder and shot if you need to reload.'

'I hope it won't come to that, but I suppose it's as well to be prepared.'

The colonel was already on his way to his horse, leaving Richard to walk beside him. 'Are you a good shot, Hadley?'

'Reasonable, but I've never fired at a man, and I hope I won't have to do so today.' The young man managed a lopsided smile. 'With luck, the appearance of my father with his sword at his side and a rifle attached to the back of his saddle should be enough to frighten them into surrender.'

There were four other men waiting to mount — they must be the reinforcements. 'God's teeth!' Guy exclaimed. 'We look like vigilantes. I'm not entirely comfortable with this escapade, Hadley, but I have to believe your father knows what he's doing.'

They mounted, and Guy almost expected Colonel Hadley to gallop down the drive like a cavalry charge, waving his sword above his head, and was relieved they trotted in a sensible manner along the snow-packed drive towards the gates. 'I assume that the colonel has reconnoitred and knows that the men we seek are still in residence?'

Hadley shrugged, the gesture barely discernible beneath his heavy riding coat. 'I've no idea. He's a military gentleman; best to leave things like this to him.'

This was hardly reassuring. Guy had no option but to speak directly to Colonel Hadley. Guy was astride a huge black gelding that suited him perfectly. He pushed it into a collected canter until he was beside the colonel. 'Tell me, sir, what sort of reception are we to expect? How many men will there be?'

'I sent somebody down yesterday to check and the villains were still there. They travel in their own carriage, with two coachmen and a couple of outriders. The innkeeper is aware that we're coming, and although he is reluctant to become involved in any violence, he will do what he can to help us evict these card sharps.'

'No doubt their presence at his hostelry is deterring his more salubrious customers, and he will be grateful that we're going to send them on their way.'

'You're probably right, Bromley. I'm hoping to avoid the necessity for violence, but I've always found it better to be prepared than otherwise.'

They slowed the pace in order to negotiate the gate. Guy was dismayed to see how deep the snow was in the lane and feared they wouldn't reach their destination without one or other of them coming to grief. They dropped to single file and allowed the horses to find their own way.

This was a white, silent world, and only the jingle of bits and the occasional snort of a horse broke the quietness. From his vantage point astride his massive gelding, Guy was able to see across the fields. Apart from the occasional column of smoke from a hidden cottage, there was nothing but snow-covered acres stretching in either direction.

No doubt everyone else had the good sense to remain inside, and only the foolhardy would be abroad in such weather. All seven of them had their faces covered by thick mufflers with only their eyes visible. Despite the bright sunshine, Guy was convinced the temperature was dropping and that it wasn't safe to be riding around the countryside when it was so cold.

The colonel stood in his stirrups and

pointed ahead. Guy did the same, and could see they were approaching the village. This was bigger than he'd expected, almost a small town. As they reached the outskirts, the snow became grey and pitted with footprints and the marks of cartwheels and horses.

'See that building just ahead?' said the colonel. 'That's our destination. We shall dismount in the yard. Smith, see that the horses are taken care of. Richard, Bromley, you come with me and try to look fearsome. The rest of you remain close and be ready to come at my call.'

Guy was unused to taking orders but said nothing — after all, a military man should know what he was doing. He dismounted and tossed the reins to the waiting Smith and then fell in behind Colonel Hadley. Young Hadley walked on his left and seemed remarkably cheerful, considering the circumstances.

'This is a bit of a lark, isn't it?' Richard said. 'I've not seen my father like this before. I can see why his regiment was so successful.'

'I'm glad that you're enjoying yourself, Hadley. I hope you still feel the same way if you're obliged to shoot somebody.'

There was no time for further conversation, as a tall, thin gentleman in a spotless apron appeared in the vestibule. 'The three of them are in the snug,' he said. 'I doubt they'll have what you want about their persons.'

'Direct me to their chamber, landlord, and I'll search whilst Colonel Hadley keeps them busy.' Guy had spoken without thought, but the suggestion was greeted enthusiastically. With some relief, he followed the landlord up the creaking staircase and along the narrow passageway into the rear of the building.

'This is the apartment, sir. Good luck with your endeavours.' The man then beat a hasty retreat, leaving Guy alone in the corridor.

Guy raised his hand to knock and then stopped. This was the first time

he'd entered anyone's apartment uninvited, and he was uncomfortable doing
so. Should he get out his pistol just in
case one of the men had returned
unnoticed? His hands were clammy and
his mouth dry. He would rather jump a
hundred giant hedges than walk into
this room. This was ridiculous — he
was Earl Bromley, so why was he
dithering about out here like a nincompoop?

He lifted the latch and charged in as
if his boots were on fire. A young man
was sitting in front of the grate, reading
a journal. His hands shot up and the
edge of the paper flew into the fire. In
seconds it was ablaze, and the flames
streaked out and caught the gentleman's coat-tails and he was engulfed.
His scream of horror rent the air.

Guy tore off his greatcoat and was
across the room in two strides. He
threw the man to the floor and then
rolled him in his coat until the flames
were doused. 'Lie still! Let me see how
badly you have been burned.'

The young man stared at him. 'I believe I'm unharmed thanks to your quick actions.'

'Allow me to assist you to your feet. I can only apologise for causing this disaster.' Guy realised he must have barged into the wrong room, as this fellow was no more a villain than he was. It was mystery to him why the landlord had directed him to this door when it was so patently obvious the occupant was not one of the men they were seeking.

His riding coat was beyond repair, but better that than the young man. He tossed the garment to one side and dropped to his knees once more in order to check that this fellow was indeed unharmed. 'You are a trifle singed, but no more than that, thank God.' He regained his feet and offered his hand. 'Bromley at your service, sir.'

'Forsyth, Jonathan. Delighted to meet you.' He pushed the chair away from the charred paper and resumed his seat as if nothing untoward had taken place.

He gestured at a similar chair opposite his and Guy took it gratefully.

'I must apologise profusely for walking unannounced into your chamber. The landlord misdirected me. I should have been in the room of the trio from London.'

Forsyth grinned. 'Actually, he didn't. I am one of those men. Are you here on behalf of the young gentleman my brothers fleeced a night or two ago?'

'I am. Colonel Hadley, the young man's father, is downstairs keeping them occupied whilst I am supposed to find the avowals and recover them.'

'There's no need to worry; I've already tossed them into the fire. My older brothers, Jack and James, are not the dyed-in-the wool villains you might have been expecting. However, they are hardened gamblers and cannot resist taking advantage of the unwary.'

'Hadley said he was held prisoner and obliged to escape through a window and abandon his horse in order to get home.'

'I'm afraid that's true, but my brothers would have released him in the morning. They were all drunk as a wheelbarrow — I collected the avowals and left them to it. As far as I understand the situation, Hadley came here to meet some friends, but they failed to turn up because of the inclement weather. We were also obliged to break our journey for the same reason.'

'Hadley painted your brothers as ghastly villains of the worst kind. I should think the situation downstairs must be rather amusing. Colonel Hadley dug out his old uniform and has charged in there waving his sabre.'

With a sigh, Forsyth stood up. 'In which case, I suppose we'd better go downstairs and make sure they have not come to blows. Too much wine and too little to do make for poor bedfellows, if you want my opinion.'

'My carriage broke its back axle, my brother broke his leg, and we sought shelter with Colonel Hadley at the Abbey. Do you have far to go in order to complete your journey?'

'We were on our way to spend a dreary few weeks with our grandparents in Norwich. They will have given up hope of seeing us by now, so there's no urgency to leave. Actually, to be frank, we all prefer it here.'

He followed Forsyth down to the dark vestibule and expected to hear raised voices, but the place was relatively quiet. He turned to his companion. 'They seem to have settled the matter amicably enough; shall we join them and see what took place? I sincerely hope that neither of your brothers caught fire.'

He was still laughing when they reached the snug. The young man pushed open the door and was greeted with enthusiasm. 'There you are, young Jonathan! We thought the earl had shot you.' The speaker was a man of about Guy's own age, immaculate in appearance, and not at all as Hadley had described him. 'I'm Jack Forsyth. That idiot over there is my younger brother James.'

Guy returned his smile and nodded politely. There was no sign of the colonel, but Hadley was deep in conversation with the man he'd supposedly come to attack.

'I understand this has been a fool's errand, Forsyth,' Guy said. 'I apologise if our appearance has discommoded you in any way.'

Hadley looked over. 'My father has gone to collect his beloved horse, and he has invited the Forsyth brothers to spend the festive season at the Abbey with us. It is the least we can do after all the upset we caused.'

'In which case, I suggest that you get your baggage and come with us immediately,' Guy said. 'The weather's deteriorating fast and soon it will be too cold to risk going outside.'

In high good humour, the three gentlemen returned to their chambers, leaving Guy alone with Richard. 'What the devil were you thinking of?' said the former. 'These are no more villains or card sharps than you are.'

The young man turned an interesting shade of beetroot and shuffled his feet like a schoolboy. 'To be honest, sir, my recollection of the evening is somewhat hazy. I knew that I'd lost a fortune, and thought that if I dressed it up a bit, my father wouldn't take it quite so badly.'

'If he's invited them to stay with us, then he cannot be too irate with you. I think we'd best get off ourselves. I'm sure they'll find their way without our guidance.'

Guy came face to face with Colonel Hadley as he was about to mount his horse. 'Bromley, I can only apologise for leading you on a wild goose chase. My son has made a laughing stock of me, and I'll not forgive him in a hurry. I intend to send him to my cousin, who is a director of the East India Company. It's high time he learned to take responsibility for his actions, and spending a year or two in India will do him good.'

1

Word spread around
garlands were being n
room, and soon Cress
group of half a dozer ......, plus
Amanda and Sarah, to help in her
endeavours. The housekeeper had obviously given permission for those who
had finished their allotted tasks to join
them.

'Excuse me, miss, but there's no
more greenery and such to use,' Polly
said cheerfully.

'That's splendid news. Thank you all
so much for giving up your free time to
make these decorations for the house.
Now all we have to do is get them hung
up, and I doubt that Grimshaw will
release any footmen from their duties to
do it.'

Chocolate and freshly baked buns
were served in the breakfast parlour for

...nd even the staff were ...nce or twice Cressida saw ...look askance at a parlourmaid ...ambermaid, but she remained ...ndly and no one was made to feel uncomfortable.

The garlands had been laid out on every available surface, and when these were full they had been put carefully along the edges of the passageways. Cook had found a bag of unused crab apples and these had been woven into the greenery, making the place smell sweet.

'I think we can be satisfied with our achievements, ladies,' Cressida said. 'All we need now is for the gentlemen to return so we can get them in place.'

'Cressie, do you have a plan, or are they to be put up randomly?' Sarah asked.

'The big kissing bough is for the ballroom, and I thought the smaller one could go in the centre of the hall. We cannot put the candles into the greenery until they are in position on the windowsills and mantelshelves.'

Amanda drained her bowl of chocolate and then picked up the empty jug and sighed with disappointment. 'I can no longer feel my toes. Why don't we retreat to somewhere warmer to discuss this?'

'It will have to be the small drawing room, as we are all far too grubby to go anywhere else. Shall I send for more chocolate and cake, Amanda?'

Cressida's suggestion was received with enthusiasm. The three girls brushed each other down and, laughing and giggling, made their way to the main part of the house. When Cressida stepped into the huge hall, she stopped in delight. 'The yule log has been brought in and is already alight. My father must have arranged it before he went out.' Although it was barely smouldering, apple logs and coal had been pushed underneath, and these were giving off a welcome warmth.

The tall-case clock struck eleven — surely the gentlemen must be home soon, as they had been gone this age. She looked around and saw that Amanda and Sarah had disappeared, and she smiled to herself. No doubt they had gone to fetch Harry in his bathchair. She hoped all this perambulating about the premises didn't set back the recovery of his leg. She stopped to arrange for further refreshments to be sent to them and then continued on her way and was unsurprised to meet the girls pushing Harry.

'Good morning, Harry,' she said. 'I'm so glad you're going to join us. We have to design a plan for our decorations and you're just the gentleman to assist with this.'

Soon they were all gathered in front of the fire, eagerly discussing how to best decorate the vast house. Cressida left the three of them to make the final decisions and wandered across to stare out of the window. From this vantage point she could see across the park to the drive. As she watched, a cavalcade of horses led by her father in his scarlet regimentals cantered into view. As he was on half pay, and had never sold his commission, she supposed he was entitled to wear them, but she thought it excessively showy on his part. Richard was trailing behind, leading the missing gelding, and Bromley was riding beside the colonel. They seemed involved in an animated conversation.

Cressida turned back to the group in front of the fire. 'The gentlemen will be here within a quarter of an hour,' she said. 'No doubt they will want something to eat, and hot drinks. Would you mind pulling the bell-strap for me, Sarah?'

As she was about to abandon her position by the window, she was astonished to see a smart travelling carriage pulled by four matching chestnuts swing into the drive. There were two on the box and two outriders. How extraordinary! Who could this second group of uninvited guests be? She spun back to the group. 'There's a carriage coming, so we have more visitors. I cannot greet them dressed as I am, so I'm going to race upstairs and change. Perhaps, Sarah, you and Amanda might like to do so as well, for we are all sadly crumpled after spending so long in the flower room.'

The girls were on their feet immediately. 'We don't have long, but if we take the back stairs we'll save a few minutes,' Sarah said. She smiled down at Harry. 'Would you mind if we abandoned you for a while?'

'Not at all. I'll get a footman to trundle me down so I can find out what happened at the inn.'

Cressida was surprised Harry knew about Richard's indiscretions, but obviously either Sarah or her brother had told him. The three of them had become bosom beaus in the short time the Bromley family had been at the Abbey.

There was no need to warn Aunt Elizabeth to change her gown, as now she had her own garments she would be immaculate in whatever she wore. Polly was waiting for Cressida, and already had hot water ready and a pretty moss-green gown draped over the end of the bed.

In less than ten minutes Cressida was changed and on her way back downstairs. As she reached the gallery, she remembered she'd not spoken to Miller; but as her maid had already been aware there were extra guests arriving, the housekeeper would be equally well-informed.

The gentlemen had exited through the front but returned through the side door that was nearest to the stables. The colonel marched, ramrod-stiff, across the hall and began to ascend the stairs two at a time. His expression was murderous, and Cressida hastily dodged into a window embrasure to avoid having to speak to him.

Bromley could reach his apartment without the necessity of coming through the hall — but her brother should be coming up to change shortly. However, although she lurked for several minutes, he didn't appear.

Something was very wrong, and the only person who could explain was Bromley, but this meant she would have to go to his apartment.

She ran round to the guest wing and could hear him talking to his valet. She knocked loudly on his bedchamber door and then retreated to the far side of the corridor. His manservant opened the door. 'I should like to speak to Lord Bromley immediately,' she said.

The man nodded, and a moment later Bromley emerged. He didn't question her visit, and pointed to the window seat at the far end of the passageway where they could sit together and talk without being overheard.

'Tell me what happened,' Cressida said. 'It's obviously something disastrous, or Papa would not be so angry.'

When Guy had explained, she was unsurprised that her father had decided to send Richard away. 'I love my brother, but one would think he was the youngest and not the oldest sibling from his behaviour. I think Papa is justified in his anger. I thank you for trying to dissuade him, but we shall have to resign ourselves to the fact that Richard will be sent to India in the spring.'

'You've taken this news remarkably well, sweetheart. I expected tears and recriminations. Will your sister be as sanguine?'

'I think so; we've both been expecting Richard to get into difficulties from which he could not be extracted easily. I think he'll benefit from a year abroad doing something useful for the family. We have interests in shipping, and no doubt he'll be involved with that.'

'I did my best to dissuade the colonel from this route, but he is adamant. After hearing what you have to say about your brother, I'm inclined to agree with your father. Are you on your way to greet your second group of uninvited guests?'

'I am, and must go down immediately. Thank you for your efforts on Richard's behalf. I can assure you they will have been much appreciated by him as well as by my sister and myself.'

Guy stood and offered to assist her to her feet, and she thought it would be churlish to refuse. The contact of his skin against hers sent a ripple of something quite unexpected up her arm. Her instinct was to snatch back her hand, but his expression held her still.

His dark eyes gazed into hers as if he were trying to see into her very soul. Then his mouth curved at the corners, and he raised her arm and dropped a playful kiss on her knuckles. Then he released her and she fled down the corridor, her emotions in turmoil. It was most vexing; her head was telling her that he was an impossible, dictatorial gentleman, whilst her heart was telling her something else entirely.

She arrived in the hall in time to greet the new guests as they stepped through the front door. 'You are very welcome, gentlemen, and I must apologise on behalf of my brother for the trouble he has caused you,' she said.

The tallest of the three, a handsome young man with green eyes and russet hair, bowed deeply. His twin brothers had the same unusual colouring but were slimmer and slightly shorter than him.

'There's no need to apologise, Miss Hadley,' he said. 'All three of them were foxed and matters got a trifle out of hand. There was no obligation for the colonel to invite us to your home, but we're very grateful. Comfortable as the hostelry is, it is hardly the place one would wish to spend the twelve days of Christmas.'

One of the twins brushed past him, shaking his head. 'Miss Hadley, I am Jack and this is James. The garrulous one is our younger brother, Jonathan Forsyth. We are absolutely thrilled to meet you.' He bowed in a rather theatrical fashion and his siblings followed suit.

The patter of female footsteps behind them meant that either Amanda or

Sarah was coming down the stairs.

'I am Sarah Hadley. We are having a pantomime, and I'll write in some parts for you.'

This unusual greeting made everyone laugh. Miller appeared and offered to personally conduct the new arrivals to their apartment, but they declined and said their men would take care of their baggage. As the main guest apartments were already in use, they would have to share accommodation in another. This had two bedchambers and only one sitting room, but was more than adequate.

Amanda arrived and introductions were made all over again. When Harry's valet wheeled him in, he exclaimed in excitement, 'Good grief! The Forsyth brothers — I've not seen you two since Oxford days. How do you come to be at the Abbey?' When he discovered these three were Richard's dastardly villains, more laughter followed.

'We cannot remain here; shall we repair to the drawing room?' Cressida suggested.

'We shall go to my rooms if you don't mind, Cressie,' Harry answered, 'as we have several years to catch up on. We'll join you for luncheon — if there's going to be any today.'

The housekeeper curtsied. 'The ladies have already eaten, my lord, so I'll have trays sent to your apartment right away.'

Jack and James escorted Harry, which left Jonathan in the hall. 'I am at your service, ladies. Is there anything you require me to do?'

'We have dozens of garlands to arrange around the house,' Cressida said. 'Would you be prepared to assist with such a mundane task?'

He bowed. 'I'd be delighted to help, Miss Hadley; and as I see Lord Bromley has arrived, no doubt he will be equally thrilled to lend a hand.'

Cressida took them to the rear of the house, where the corridors were filled with greenery and the flower room stacked high with wreaths and beribboned garlands. Both gentlemen were suitably impressed at their industry.

Sarah fetched her plan, and before long three footmen joined them, but Richard was conspicuously absent. The small potted bay trees were positioned on either side of doorways, and the two kissing boughs were hung by the footmen, who were well used to ascending stepladders in order to dust the chandeliers and replace the candles.

Lady Bromley came to admire what was being done, but didn't offer to help and drifted off to the library to fetch a book — at least that was what she said she was doing. Richard eventually came down, and soon after that the Forsyth twins appeared, eager to take part in the fun.

When the final candle had been pushed into the last garland, Cressida was delighted. 'We must light the candles in order to see how pretty everything looks.'

'Allow me, Cressida — you must stand in the centre of the hall, where you will get the best view,' Guy said, removing the taper from her hand.

He moved smoothly from one garland to another, and although she should have been admiring the greenery, Cressida's eyes remained fixed firmly on him. The rest of the party had drifted away — the Forsyth brothers had gone to their room to change for dinner while Sarah, Richard, Amanda and Harry were closeted together, writing the extra parts for the new guests.

When the final candle was alight, Guy tossed the end of the taper into the fireplace in which the yule log was burning merrily, then strolled across to join Cressida. Slowly she spun round, admiring their joint handiwork. The Abbey had never looked so lovely. Even as a child, she couldn't remember there being so many beautiful arrangements.

'Thank you, Bromley. You are quite right to tell me to remain here. It's the perfect place to admire the decorations.'

He didn't answer, but stepped dangerously close. 'It also positions you directly under the mistletoe.'

Before she could react, he placed one arm around her waist, and the other slid up her back until it was resting lightly on her hair. She was aware of his chest pressing against her bosom, and of his hard thighs close to hers. She raised both hands until they were resting on his waistcoat, intending to push him away, but her fingers could feel the heavy thumping of his heart. Was she causing it to beat like this?

'Look at me, sweetheart.'

She knew she shouldn't, but couldn't help herself. As soon as her face tilted, his eyes blazed and his arms tightened. Then his lips were on hers and she forgot everything she'd ever been told about correct behaviour and gave herself up to the exquisite sensation.

Too soon, Guy raised his head and gently held her at arm's length. She'd expected an immediate declaration of love, perhaps an offer of marriage, but got neither. Instead he scanned her face for a few seconds, raised her hands and kissed her knuckles, and then with a heart-stopping smile released her and bounded up the stairs, having not said a word about his reprehensible behaviour.

Then she realised she had brought it upon herself by standing under the kissing bough. This was the only time a gentleman could kiss a lady without fear of damaging her reputation. A delicious warmth rippled through her as she touched her swollen lips. For some strange reason she was not offended or shocked by Bromley's behaviour, but thrilled he'd found her attractive enough to risk being trapped into marriage.

There was only half an hour before the dinner gong would be struck, and if she didn't hurry she would be tardy.

★　★　★

Guy felt like punching the air or turning somersaults but wisely refrained. As soon as his lips had touched hers, he knew he'd made the right choice. Cressida was the perfect match for him, and he was determined to speak to the colonel before the night was out and ask his permission to pay his addresses.

His first marriage had been with the daughter of family friends. Charlotte was quiet, respectful and with an impeccable pedigree — everything a man in his position required for a suitable wife. Their union had been happy, and love had grown over the years. Their only sadness had been the lack of children. Guy had genuinely mourned her death, but had always known that one day he would have to marry again. Only now did he understand that he'd never been in love with Charlotte — he'd loved her, but more like a sister than a lover. He'd never felt this blaze of passion, this uncontrollable urge to spend every waking minute with her that he'd been experiencing since he'd met Cressida.

She was so far from his idea of an

ideal partner that he couldn't understand how he'd fallen irrevocably in love with her, and in so short a time. She was maddeningly argumentative, treated him with contempt, had no respect for his position, and was quite prepared to put him in his place. At first sight he'd not seen her beauty, but now he knew she was a diamond of the first water and outshone every other woman of his acquaintance. Marriage to her would be exhilarating, exciting and exasperating. All he had to do was convince her she would be his perfect countess.

15

Cressida was determined not to be the last to arrive this evening. She scarcely noticed what Polly had put out for her to wear, so keen was her desire to be downstairs in advance of the rest of the house party. There would be a surfeit of gentlemen around the table, and she wondered how the diners would arrange themselves.

Her heart skipped a beat as, with her skirts held out of danger, she ran down the stairs. The drawing room was occupied, but not by the person she most wanted to see. Her father was staring miserably into the roaring fire. 'Papa, I'm glad we can have a few moments together before everyone else arrives. I gather Richard is once more in disgrace.'

He turned, and she was shocked to see tears in his eyes. 'I must send him away; I have no choice. But it will break my heart to do so. Your brother is a trifle wild, but no more than I was at his age.'

'You, wild? I thought you in the army while still a youth.'

His expression lightened a little. 'There's plenty of opportunity for a young ensign to get into mischief — especially in peacetime, as it was when I joined. I was almost cashiered and threatened with a flogging, despite being an officer, before I settled down.'

'Then it's a great shame Richard didn't want to follow in your footsteps. It's going to be hard especially for Sarah, who is inordinately close to him; but his behaviour will only get worse unless he's forced to take on some responsibility. After this debacle, I agree with you that Richard must go, for I can see no other way to remedy the situation.'

Her father's smile was sad, but he nodded and held out his hand. She moved across and took it, and he gathered her close and for a moment they embraced. She could not remember the last time this had happened. 'Thank you for your support, my dear. I might not say it often enough, but you make this place a home for all of us. Your mother would be proud of you.'

'Does Richard know his fate? I've not seen him since he got back from the village.'

'I told him immediately. Once he's had time to digest the unpalatable information, he'll accept my decision and not sulk.'

They moved apart, and he looked a little more cheerful now. 'Do you like Lady Bromley?' he asked suddenly.

Somewhat startled by the abrupt change of subject, and at a loss to know why he'd asked this question, for a moment Cressida couldn't think of an appropriate answer. Finally she replied, 'Yes, of course I do. Indeed, I must own that I have become fond of all of them, despite my initial dislike of Lord Bromley.'

'It was a lucky day indeed that their carriage broke its axle outside our property.'

A cheerful voice replied from the far end of the drawing room. Harry had been wheeled in by his friends through the doors that led directly into the passageway nearest to his apartment. 'Apart from my having a broken leg, Colonel Hadley, I would heartily concur. And who would have thought my two closest friends from university would find themselves marooned so close?'

After the usual greetings, the colonel joined the group, and they were soon busy discussing the merits of his favourite hunter — the one that Richard had borrowed without permission and been forced to abandon.

A footman came in through a hidden entrance in the panelling, holding a silver tray upon which were glasses brimming with an assortment of beverages. There was sweet sherry wine, ratafia and orgeat, but none of them were to Cressida's liking. She would wait and have wine with her meal.

Guy strolled in, looking magnificent in his evening black, a single diamond pin holding his intricately tied neckcloth in place. He had adopted the new fashion of pantaloons instead of knee breeches and stockings, and they served to emphasise his length of leg.

He bowed and walked directly to Cressida with the glint of something she didn't recognise in his eyes. 'Good evening, my love,' he said. 'You look quite beautiful tonight. That is a delightful confection and a most unusual colour.'

She glanced at her evening gown. 'Thank you. I believe the colour is called *eau de nil*.' She smiled confidingly. 'I scarcely noticed what I put on this evening, I was in such a hurry to get ready. Until you mentioned it, I hadn't realised I was wearing this particular ensemble.'

Guy's laughter attracted the attention of the others, and he was obliged to explain what he had found so amusing. Aunt Elizabeth had drifted in, in a gown of purple diaphanous material that suited her to perfection, and she joined in the merriment.

'Cressida, I believe you must be the only young lady in Christendom who could have said such a thing. I cannot imagine anyone else appearing in a gown they couldn't describe down to the last bugle bead or rouleau.'

'You look enchanting, Miss Hadley; and if there is to be dancing, I shall be the first to ask you to stand up with me,' Jack — or it could be James — said gallantly. Cressida could not tell one from the other and thought they dressed identically in order to confuse people.

'Dancing? I don't see why we shouldn't roll back the carpet and have a reel or two after dinner,' the colonel said.

'Unless Amanda or Aunt Elizabeth can play, I shall be obliged to refuse your request, Mr Forsyth,' Cressida said.

Harry chipped in, 'It would not do to deprive the many gentlemen present of your company, Cressie. You're forgetting that I am proficient on the pianoforte, and will be delighted to play so everyone can dance.'

The last four members of their party arrived together. The youngest Forsyth brother looked older than his years now he was in evening dress. Sarah looked as beautiful as always, and Amanda was her match. Richard appeared unbothered by his imminent banishment and looked equally splendid.

Grimshaw announced that dinner was served, and there was the usual melee that always took place when there was more than family present. Cressida hung back, not wishing to be crushed by the bathchair, and found that Guy had chosen to do the same. He offered his arm; she willingly placed her hand on it, and they entered the dining room together. Her father and his mother had taken the two seats at the head of the table. Amanda, Richard and Sarah were sitting together on one side and Harry and the new arrivals on the other. This left the only other seats vacant at the other end of the table.

Guy waved away an attentive footman and moved out a chair for Cressida himself. Once she was seated, he joined her and positioned his chair in a way that meant he was so close his arm would brush hers when he reached for anything; and his thigh was dangerously close to hers too.

This was going to be an interesting dinner, and not just for her. The centre of the polished table was occupied by a delightful arrangement of greenery and red, green and gold bows of silken ribbon. The sideboard and the mantelshelf were also dressed in Christmas finery, and the best crystal and silverware had been used tonight.

The colonel waited until everyone had settled and their glasses were full before raising his hand for silence. 'Tomorrow is the eve of our saviour's birthday, and this is the first time for many years that I can say I'm eagerly anticipating the twelve days of Christmas. The Abbey looks beautiful, and Lady Bromley and I have arranged for a series of enjoyable activities to take place on each day.' He gestured towards the Forsyth brothers. 'Thank you for agreeing to join us; it is now a merry house party indeed.'

A chorus of agreement rippled around the table, and when they raised their glasses to drink a toast to the forthcoming celebration Bromley's sleeve brushed Cressida's arm at exactly the place where her elbow-length gloves finished and there was an expanse of bare skin. Her chair was jammed against his, and he'd surreptitiously moved an empty chair so that she was effectively held captive. What was he thinking of? If she was to spend the entire meal trying to avoid touching or being touched by him, her enjoyment of the delicious food and jolly company would be quite spoilt.

She swivelled in her chair in order to be able to see him properly, and when he didn't look in her direction she stamped on his foot, causing his hand to jerk. This got his full attention.

'Oh dear! It must be irksome becoming so decrepit one cannot avoid spilling one's wine into one's lap.' She smiled sweetly at him, and she was almost certain she could hear his teeth grinding. This must be like baiting a bear at a circus. Exciting, but fraught with danger.

'I gather that you wish to speak to me. How can I be of assistance?' His tone was even, but she could not help but be aware of his tension as he was pressed so closely to her.

'As you can see, I am unable to move freely because by some strange mischance our chairs are far too close together. Could I ask you to remove yourself six inches along the table so that we might both enjoy our dinner without fear of another accident?'

For a moment she thought he might refuse, but then he smiled and, with a slight nod as if acknowledging her victory, he stood up and moved his chair the required distance. Fortunately everyone else was busy helping themselves to the first course, which had so many removes that Cressida was sure she would never get round to tasting everything.

Now that Guy was a safe distance from her, she was able to relax and enjoy the unusual sight of the table full of guests. Papa never entertained in the evenings, and only occasionally did he invite the neighbours for a garden party or some such thing. From the magnificent spread that Cook had provided, she rather thought she wasn't the only one excited at the prospect of having a houseful. With the seven extra guests had come three valets, two ladies' maids and a dozen outside men, all of whom had to be fed and accommodated. There were also eight extra horses and two grooms to feed in the stables.

The Abbey, so-called because it had been built on the ruins of an actual religious building a hundred years ago, could accommodate another dozen visitors if they were prepared to sleep in the less commodious guestrooms on the nursery floor. Ideally a carriage with three unattached young ladies should arrive to make the numbers even. But Cressida smiled at her silliness. Having two uninvited sets of guests was unheard of; to have a third would be taking a coincidence too far.

Guy leaned across and removed the plate from in front of her and proceeded to fill it with a variety of tasty morsels. She was quite capable of selecting her own dinner, but she rather liked being taken care of. Usually she was the one doing the caring.

'There, sweetheart, you have a little of everything that is within our reach. If you require anything else, I shall ask for it to be passed down to you.'

'Thank you, but there is more than enough on my plate. There is a second course before the desserts and I wish to leave room for those.'

'I don't believe I've seen a better dinner anywhere. Indeed, I think this surpasses anything we've had at Bromley Court.'

His words were overheard by his mother, who must have been paying particular attention to her son at that moment, as he had not been speaking especially loudly. 'Bromley, I'm surprised to hear you say such a thing about our own table. When we entertain, we have as many courses and removes as they have here, and they are equally delicious.' She gestured with her fork to her other children, expecting them to confirm her statement.

Amanda was deep in conversation with Richard and didn't hear her. However, Harry immediately responded. 'Mama, shall we allow that both dinner at the Abbey and at Bromley Court are equally superb?' He fixed his older brother with a piercing stare. 'When the Hadley family come for an extended stay in the spring, they will find out for themselves.'

It was as if the entire table held its

breath whilst they waited for Guy to respond to this challenge. He looked directly at the colonel. 'Colonel Hadley, I have already extended an invitation to Cressida, but I shall make this an official request. I would be honoured if you and your family would care to join us next year.'

Now the attention turned to Cressida's father, as she and her siblings knew that he had as much enthusiasm for visits as he did for entertaining. However, he nodded and smiled. 'We should be delighted to accept your kind invitation, my lord. I expect that you are in London for the Season.'

'We are, sir. We have a house in Grosvenor Square, and would be pleased if you would care to join us there before coming to Hertfordshire.'

Lady Bromley touched the colonel's arm, and he looked down at her. 'Do come, Colonel Hadley. I don't believe that either of your girls has had a Season, and I should be thrilled to sponsor them alongside Amanda.'

This was a step too far. He shook his head politely. 'I thank you for your kind offer, but Richard will be abroad by then, and I do not go to London anymore. However, if my girls were to accept your invitation, then they may do so with my approval.'

Sarah looked horrified at the suggestion, and Cressida stepped in. 'Neither Sarah nor I are overfond of London, but we thank you for your offer. However, we should be delighted to visit Bromley Court when you return from Town.'

The conversation moved on to other less contentious topics while the first course was taken away. There was so much left, Cressida knew the staff would eat well that evening. Eventually it was time for her to lead the ladies into the drawing room and leave the gentlemen to their port.

'Cressida, my dear, will we be able to attend church on Christmas morning if the weather is so inclement?' asked Lady Bromley.

'Although you cannot see it behind the trees, Aunt Elizabeth, the church is no more than half a mile from here, and we can walk there even in the snow.'

They had barely seated themselves by the fire when two footmen slipped in and began to roll up the carpet at the far end of the room. Cressida had quite forgotten the Forsyth brothers' determination to dance and Harry's offer to play the piano. She jumped to her feet. 'I'd better find some music that will be suitable for a Scottish reel, a country dance and perhaps a cotillion.'

'Do you have anything we could waltz to, Cressie?' Amanda asked eagerly.

Cressida looked at Lady Bromley for approval of this suggestion. The waltz was considered a rather rackety dance, and unattached young ladies were not expected to participate. 'Would you have any objection if we waltzed?'

'Not at all, my dear, for the usual rules don't apply at a family gathering. I might even take to the floor myself if you can find music that will suit this dance.'

* * *

Guy refused the port when it was pushed round to him. He'd had more than enough claret already and didn't wish to cloud his senses. 'Harry, are you still willing to play so the rest of us can dance?'

Harry hid his smile — he understood that the request was made so that Guy could partner Cressida, and that he didn't give a damn what anyone else did. 'If there's music, then I can play. As neither of us is drinking, perhaps you would care to wheel me through so I can get organised.'

Guy was on his feet immediately and nodded to the remainder of the party. 'If you will excuse us, gentlemen, we will see you in the drawing room in due course.' He whisked his brother through the double doors and almost upended the bathchair in his hurry to exit.

'Hey, steady on, old chap — you nearly had me out. At the risk of you planting me a facer, I'd like to add that Cressie is perfect for you. When do you intend to make her an offer?'

'Not before I've spoken to her father, but I'm certain she knows in which direction the wind is blowing and feels the same way as I do about the prospect of a match between us.'

'I don't think you're the only one with marriage on your mind. Have you noticed how cosy the colonel and Mama are getting?'

'I'd have to be blind not to have done so,' Guy said. 'Personally I think it would be an unmitigated disaster. He is a serious man and has not a romantic bone in his body, whereas our parent has feathers for brains and thinks of nothing but frivolity and the latest fashions.'

His brother shrugged. 'I fear you're correct, Bromley. But you know Mama — once she sets her sights on something, she doesn't give in easily.'

The sound of chairs scraping back in the dining room added wings to Guy's heels. He'd no intention of allowing any of the Forsyth brothers to claim a dance with his intended bride. He and Harry erupted into the drawing room, and he was unable to prevent the bathchair colliding with two footmen who were crouching over a rolled-up carpet.

16

Bromley's spectacular entrance had all the ladies on their feet. Cressida was relieved that poor Harry, who was almost catapulted from his chair, managed to save himself from what could have been a damaging fall. She wasn't sure whether she should laugh or be concerned. Bromley was sprawled inelegantly on the boards, and the unfortunate footmen were in no better state.

'Dammit, Bromley, that was a close thing,' Harry exclaimed as his brother began to disentangle the chair from the roll of carpet. 'Wouldn't fancy my chances if I'd come out of this.'

The earl grinned at his sibling, but quickly turned his attention to the servants who had been sent flying. 'I beg your pardon; I hope I didn't hurt you. I should know better than to play tomfool at my age.' He leaned down and heaved the first of the men to his feet, but when he turned to assist the second he was already upright. Their wigs were askew and their appearance somewhat shuffled, but apart from that they were perfectly fine. They bowed and then quickly tidied themselves as the dreaded Grimshaw, hearing the commotion, had come to investigate.

'No harm done, my lord,' he said. 'All in a day's work.' The servants hastily dragged the carpet out of sight and then vanished before the butler could reprimand them. Bromley waved the man away and turned his attention to the group of interested spectators, of whom Cressida was one.

'Well, I hope you enjoyed the entertainment, for I can give you my word I'll not be doing anything of a similar nature again.'

She had been about to enquire what had prompted him to gallop about the place like a schoolboy, when the remainder of the gentlemen arrived.

Harry had asked to be positioned in front of the piano and was ready to play as soon as dancers took the floor.

'I've given my brother instructions to play a waltz, sweetheart,' Guy said. 'I hope you are cognisant of the steps, as I've no wish to be made to look foolish.'

She laughed out loud and he pretended to be cross. He also kept his bulk between her and the Forsyth brothers, making sure they didn't get a chance to ask her to dance with one of them. He led her out onto the boards and she noticed that Richard had claimed Amanda, Sarah was with one of the Forsyth twins, and to her astonishment her father was leading out Lady Bromley. This would be the first time any member of the family had seen him attempt to dance, and Cressida feared he would make a complete cake of himself.

Her dismay must have been apparent from her face. 'Don't look so worried, Cressida,' her father said. 'I was an officer in Wellington's army and he expected us to be able to acquit ourselves well on the dance floor when we attended any social function.'

This comment was bellowed at parade-ground level, and her cheeks coloured. Instead of being shocked by his shouting across the drawing room, his partner laughed gaily and moved swiftly into his arms, ready for the music to start. When it began, she was swept away and had never experienced anything like it before. Guy was not just proficient, he was an expert. She was guided smoothly around the floor, and he made her feel as if she weighed nothing at all.

She closed her eyes and allowed the music and the delightful sensation of being held in a gentleman's arms to transport her to a place where she'd never expected to go. Up until this point she'd considered dancing more of a chore than a pleasure; but judging by the expression on her sister's face, she too was now enjoying the waltz.

'Look at me, Cressida,' said Guy. 'I

want to see your face whilst you're in my arms.'

She ignored his command, but her lips curved. 'I prefer to keep my eyes shut; then I can imagine I'm dancing with Prince Charming at the palace ball.'

His hold tightened. 'Are you suggesting, my love, that you would prefer to be dancing with a fairy-tale character instead of a real earl?'

Now she did look at him, and an unaccountable tightness afflicted her bodice. 'An earl is all very well, but any young lady of character would much prefer to be swept off her feet by a prince.' She flicked her eyelashes at him in what she hoped was a flirtatious manner. 'However, I will admit that I'd much prefer to be in your arms than in the arms of the Prince Regent.'

'Tarnation take it! I should hope so too. I intend to dance every dance with you tonight. No, don't poker up at me — the rules don't apply at a private party.'

The music ended and they were forced to stop. Everyone congratulated Harry on his performance, and he immediately launched into another piece suitable for the waltz. Cressida saw the younger Forsyth heading purposefully in her direction and tried to step away from Guy. He was having nothing of it, however; and before she could protest or accept the invitation of another partner, she was in his arms once more and lost to everything else.

'Bromley, I've no wish to be monopolised by anyone. There are only four ladies, and six gentlemen who wish to dance, so I must make myself available. I am the hostess here and cannot ignore the wishes of my other guests by giving you precedence.'

'Not give me precedence when I am the most important fellow here? Remember, I think myself a grand gentleman far above the touch of these common people. You should be honoured . . . '

She was laughing so much she forgot

the steps, but he merely lifted her from the floor and continued to dance. 'Bromley, you are absurd. Put me down at once.'

Her slippers were back on the boards, and they continued in perfect harmony around the floor until the dance was done. This time Cressida was ready and nimbly skipped away from him, and with a teasing smile accepted the hand of Jonathan Forsyth.

'I'm going to play a country dance,' Harry informed them. 'We don't have the requisite number of couples, but I'm sure you'll manage.'

Jonathan prepared to lead Cressida to the head of the set, but she shook her head. 'I'm no expert at the figures,' she said. 'I think Amanda would be better leading.'

'Thank you, but I should like to lead. I shall keep the figures simple so you can copy them easily.' One of the Forsyth twins was partnering Amanda this time, and Richard and Bromley were the wallflowers. Papa had not relinquished his partner, and they took the second place. Sarah and the other twin were next, and Cressida and Jonathan took the end position. By the time it was their turn to dance, Cressida was confident she could manage the steps without embarrassing herself. The dancing continued until the supper tray came in, and by then she had partnered everyone apart from her own family.

She noticed Bromley talking to his brother and saw Harry nod vigorously. What mischief were they planning now? Her feet were quite sore after all the activity, but she could not recall having had so much fun in her life before.

By right she should have presided over the tea urn, but Lady Bromley was already there, and Cressida was happy to let things remain as they were. However, Guy was not so sanguine.

'I apologise for my parent, Cressida. She has usurped your position, and I'm most displeased.'

'Please don't be cross on my account.

We stand on no ceremony here. Indeed, I am only too happy to collapse in this chair and have you wait upon me. I should like a little of everything from the supper table, as well as a dish of tea.'

Guy swept her a ridiculous bow. 'I am yours to command, my love.'

Whilst she waited, she gazed around the drawing room and saw that her sister was sitting with Harry, her father was with Aunt Elizabeth, and the three Forsyth brothers were helping themselves at the buffet table — but there was no sign of Amanda or Richard.

Cressida's stomach lurched. If Guy realised they had gone off somewhere alone together, the evening would be ruined. She walked swiftly over to Sarah and whispered in her ear, 'Do you know where Richard and Amanda have gone?'

Her sister shook her head and stood up. 'We must find them immediately. Amanda is an impressionable girl and could well be led into a compromising position. Do you think Richard might be trying to trick her into marriage so he doesn't have to leave?'

'I sincerely hope not. Our brother is a trifle wild, but he'd not do anything so underhand. I'm certain this is merely an innocent excursion, but Bromley will be furious, and I've no wish for the party to be spoiled. I'll check the ballroom. Sarah, would you go in the other direction?'

The passageway was chill after the warmth of the drawing room, and she shivered as she ran to the ballroom. This was a fool's errand, as the chamber was unlit and obviously unoccupied. Cressida spun, intending to search elsewhere, and collided with a solid wall of flesh.

Guy's quick reactions saved her from a tumble. 'What in God's name are you doing out here? Is something wrong?'

She blurted the words out: 'My brother has gone somewhere with Amanda.'

He put his jacket around her

shoulders before answering. 'You were searching in the wrong direction, darling. They are in the entrance hall under the kissing bough.'

'I should have thought of that myself. Richard can be foolhardy. He's in enough trouble without upsetting anyone else.'

'I can hardly object to him kissing my sister under the mistletoe, as I've done the same thing myself.'

She couldn't resist. 'Why did you wish to kiss Amanda?'

His arm encircled her waist and drew her possessively to his side. 'I'm not going to remain here in the cold bandying words with you, young lady. We shall return at once to the drawing room, where you are to remain until I give you leave to go.'

She couldn't object to his words, as they were accompanied by an affection-ate kiss on the top of her head. However, she did intend to insist he cease to lard his conversation with unsuit-able endearments. 'Bromley, I am neither your sweetheart nor your darling.'

'Are you not? I think you have it wrong, my love, as I rather think you are.'

Guy watched her expression change from puzzlement to realisation. This wasn't the time or the place he'd intended to propose, but he had no choice. Gently he took her shoulders and turned her to face him. When he had her full attention, he reached inside the folds of the jacket she was wearing draped across her shoulders and took her hands. Then he dropped to one knee, keeping her hands within his.

'Cressida, my darling — I know we've only been acquainted for a few days, but I've fallen totally, head over heels in love with you. Would you do me the incredible honour of becoming my next countess?'

For a dreadful moment he thought she was about to shake her head, but then her eyes widened and her smile was radiant. 'I know it's quite extraordinary, but I too have been afflicted in the same way. Although my head is telling me to wait, my heart is saying yes.' She tugged at his hands. 'Please get up now. I've no wish for anyone to find you on your knees in front of me.'

He was on his feet in a trice and closed the gap between them so he could seal the bargain with a kiss. Being so close to her made him as foolish as a schoolboy in the throes of his first infatuation. Then her last remark filtered into his befuddled brain. 'Why didn't you want me to be seen making you an offer?'

'I don't want anyone to know we are betrothed.'

'Whyever not? Are you afraid your father will refuse his consent?'

'I am. He tells me every day that he cannot manage without me, and I fear if we spring this on him he will react badly to the announcement.'

'When will you reach your majority?'

'Not for another year, but I don't think I could bear to wait that long.'

This was the sort of thing Guy wanted to hear, and it reassured him.

'I've no wish to antagonise him any further. Although we're jogging along amicably at the moment, the tension is just below the surface, and it wouldn't take much to have us at loggerheads again.' Cressida smiled so sweetly at him that his annoyance melted. 'What do you wish me to do, sweetheart? I think it might become patently obvious we're involved, and wouldn't it be even worse if the colonel believed I was toying with your affections?'

'I shall flirt outrageously with all the single gentlemen and then he will not be any the wiser. We must make sure we find ourselves unexpectedly underneath the mistletoe on as many occasions as possible in the next few days.'

This suggestion was not to Guy's liking at all. 'You will do no such thing. I am your future husband, even if the matter has not been announced formally, and you will behave with due decorum.' No sooner had he spoken than he regretted his pomposity, but it was too late to retract.

300

Her expression changed from loving to frosty. 'Until you have spoken to my father and gained his permission, my lord, I shall do as I please, and it is no business of yours how I behave.'

She shrugged his jacket onto the floor and stalked off with her head in the air. Elation to dejection in the space of a few moments — and it was all his own fault. He snatched up his discarded jacket and pushed his arms through the sleeves, wishing he'd not had it made quite so close-fitting. Eventually he was correctly dressed again and ready to rejoin the party.

He'd abandoned his supper when he'd seen Cressida rush off, and someone else had taken it. He stared at the depleted buffet table with disfavour. There was nothing left to tempt him, and he had never been a tea drinker. There must be brandy somewhere; he'd find himself a decanter and glass and go and sulk in solitude. He was being ridiculous and must put matters right between them at once.

Cressida was sitting with the Forsyth brothers, apparently unconcerned by their disagreement. Guy leaned against the wall and stared at her until she glanced his way. He gestured towards the far end of the room where there was a window seat, and then strolled off in that direction, praying she would join him and not remain angry.

A few minutes later she was at his side, her expression anxious and no sign of her former annoyance present. 'Is something wrong? Surely you didn't take my comments seriously? You must understand that I am given to exaggeration and hyperbole. I've never flirted with anyone and don't intend to start now.'

'I wanted to apologise for my crass remark. I've become overfond of telling my family how to behave, and it's going to take me time to adjust to having someone in my life who does not think I belong on a pedestal.'

'*I* shall try not to be so outspoken in future if *you* will promise not to scowl at me so readily.'

It took all Guy's self-control not to take her into his arms and kiss her breathless. 'I love you, Cressida Hadley. Even when I look at my most forbidding, that will never change. We shall keep our betrothal a secret between us for now — but whatever the consequences, I intend to speak to your father before we leave.'

'Thank you; I appreciate your understanding. What are we to do if he refuses?'

'Never fear, sweetheart. I give you my word you will be my wife by the summer of next year.'

'Shall we elope? How romantic. Will you climb to my bedchamber window so that I may escape down the ladder with you?'

'I'd rather have my teeth pulled than do anything so ridiculous. We shall be married, here or at the family chapel at Bromley Court, with all due ceremony, and our friends and family present. Then I shall take you on a wedding tour to wherever you wish.'

'I've never been abroad at all, and now that we are at peace with France I should dearly love to go to Paris, Venice and anywhere in between.'

Harry struck up a chord on the pianoforte. Guy bowed and held out his hand. 'I believe this is my waltz, sweetheart, and I don't give a damn if it's a monstrous breach of etiquette to dance with you again.'

17

Cressida knew it would be fruitless to protest and willingly joined him on the temporary dance floor. After all, if their parents were happy to dance every dance together, then why should she cavil? The tempo of this waltz was slower than the previous two and allowed her to relax into Bromley's arms — no, in future he would be Guy to her, and he would just have to adjust to the shock of being addressed by his given name.

This was the final dance, and afterward the party broke up. The Forsyth brothers insisted on ferrying Harry back to his apartment so they could indulge in further drinking. Richard escorted Amanda to the guest staircase and then headed in the same direction as his new friends. Lady Bromley had already gone up, and no doubt the colonel was having a final snifter in his study. Cressida was reluctant to end what had been a wonderful evening, and one she would never forget.

Guy was lounging in the doorway and nodded towards the kissing bough. She couldn't resist and hurried across to position herself directly underneath. He was at her side in seconds, and when he eventually lifted his head her knees were weak and she was giddy with excitement.

She tilted her head and smiled. 'I've come to a momentous decision, my love.'

'Do go on, sweetheart. I've a strong feeling I'm not going to like this one bit.'

'In future I shall address you as Guy, and I don't care if you dislike it. I'm to be your wife next year and have no intention of calling my husband by anything but his given name.'

His hand cupped her face and he lowered his head to kiss her tenderly.

'Can I ask a small favour? Will you only use it when we are alone together? I've no wish for anyone else to adopt this familiarity.'

With a deep sigh of contentment, she dropped her head on his chest, loving the feel of his hard strength against her soft curves. As they stood there, the clock struck midnight. 'It's now Christmas Eve,' Cressida said, 'and tomorrow will be our Lord's birthday. In this family we don't give gifts to each other, but only to the staff. Of course, we put a substantial amount in the poor box on Christmas Day.' She couldn't prevent a large yawn from escaping and immediately apologised for her poor manners.

'Time you retired, sweetheart. I shall not offer to escort you to your chamber, as I doubt I would have the strength of character to remain on the correct side of the door.'

'Good night, Guy, my love. I shall be counting the days until we can be together all the time.'

His eyes darkened with that familiar

look, and she knew it was time to go before something happened that they would both regret. From the safety of the stairs she turned to wave, but he was no longer there. For a big man, he moved silently and swiftly — another thing she must file away for future reference.

★ ★ ★

Her first task the next morning was to examine Harry's leg to ensure that it had suffered no setback after all his activity the previous day. Satisfied the limb was healing well, she left him to get dressed. They would all meet here after breakfast for a morning of rehearsing the pantomime.

As she left the chamber, she met Guy leaving his, and without conscious thought she flew into his arms. A satisfactory few minutes later he stepped away. 'Is my brother flourishing?'

'Indeed he is. I shall issue him with his crutches tomorrow so he can move himself about the place. However, I don't think he will be able to accompany us to church, as the bathchair will not navigate the path and he could not possibly make his way so far on crutches.'

'Don't look so despondent, sweetheart. I'm sure Harry will survive. Apart from the morning being spent rehearsing this pantomime, what else has been planned for our entertainment?'

'I think we are to play a variety of card games, and then there is to be a full dress rehearsal in the ballroom before dinner.'

She stopped as they entered the grand hall, breathing in the festive scent of spices and applewood logs. 'Doesn't it smell delicious? Cook must have spared some of her precious cinnamon and sprinkled it on the log.'

'Everything about this place is magical,' Guy agreed. 'This will be a Christmas neither of us will ever forget. We can tell our children and grandchildren how we met and that fate stepped in to throw us together.'

The sun was out, and shards of light patterned the chequered floor, making the surface dance. Guy was right — the Abbey this Christmas was a place of enchantment. They strolled companionably to the breakfast parlour, and Cressida was unsurprised to find it already occupied. Harry and the Forsyth brothers were at the table, tucking into laden plates. She raised her hand to prevent them from standing as was expected. 'Remain seated, gentlemen. In this house we are less formal. Has anyone been outside today?'

Guy spoke from beside her. 'I have. I believe it's a little warmer today, which is a good thing, but it could herald further snow.'

There was a lively discussion about the possibility of more snow, which continued unabated after the remainder of the party arrived.

'As I am now more mobile, I suggest we have our rehearsal in the ballroom, where we're going to perform on Boxing Day,' Harry said.

'I have set the footmen to painting the scenery, and I believe that the costumes will be done in good time for the dress rehearsal later today,' Sarah told them.

The air positively crackled with excitement, and even the colonel appeared to be affected by this most unusual Christmas. Cressida decided she would see how he was after the dress rehearsal; and if he remained in such ebullient humour, she would ask Guy to speak to him. She hated having secrets from her sister, but until Papa had given his permission her betrothal must remain a secret.

★   ★   ★

The rehearsal went as smoothly as it could have done, considering who the participants were. The older members of the party had failed to learn their lines, saying they could read them from

311

the script or make them up as they went along.

Guy was surprisingly good as the king, and the extra parts written for the new arrivals made the pantomime even sillier than it had been before. At midday Harry called a halt. 'I think this is as good as it's going to get. We shall have a final run-through in costume and then forget about the pantomime until Boxing Day. I'm going to practise using my crutches, so I can make my own way to dinner this evening.'

They dispersed in high spirits, and Cressida heard Richard challenging the Forsyth brothers to a game of billiards. No doubt gambling would be involved, but she hoped they had all learnt their lesson after the debacle at the inn a few nights ago.

She was about to make her way to the small dining room when her father waylaid her. 'I need to speak to you, my dear. Would you mind coming to my study before you go for your repast?'

Had he discovered her secret? He

didn't seem at all angry, but he was a trifle agitated, winch was not like him at all. She followed him to his study, and he closed the door firmly behind them.

'I expect you know what it is I wish to speak to you about, my dear.'

She nodded. 'I do, Papa. I guessed as soon as you asked me to come with you.'

'Are you happy about it? You have no doubts or reservations on the matter? Such a decision normally takes months rather than days.'

'Of course I'm happy, but I'm surprised that you have made no objections to the marriage.'

'Objections? The decision was mine, not Elizabeth's. I understand that she is quite different from your mama . . . '

'Papa, we are talking at cross purposes. Are you telling me that you have made Lady Bromley an offer?'

He stared at her as if she were an escapee from Bedlam. 'Of course I am. What did you think I meant?' Then his expression changed as realisation dawned.

'You and Bromley? Devil take it — the man has not had the good manners to speak to me before making you an offer.'

'I asked him not to speak to you until the New Year.'

'Then he should have ignored your instructions. I don't like the man; I'll not give my consent. You will have to wait until you reach your majority to tie yourself to that jackanapes.'

She spoke without thought for the consequences. 'If you marry Lady Bromley, don't expect me to remain under the same roof as the two of you. She would turn the household upside down, and has you on leading strings already. I'll not stay here and have my beloved mama's position usurped.'

His hand struck her across the cheek before she had time to move. She reeled back, clutching her face. Then her head cracked against the wall and her world went black.

* * *

Guy was in his shirtsleeves when there was a thunderous knocking on the door of his bedchamber. He was across the room before his valet could react. He flung it open to find his mother, her face tear-streaked and her complexion as pale as a sheet.

'Bromley, you must come at once. This is my fault — I should never have agreed. He has killed her and stormed out of the house, and nobody knows what to do.'

Guy was on his way in seconds, guessing at once what his mother's garbled comments referred to. If that bastard had harmed a hair on his beloved's head, he would swing for him. Downstairs pandemonium reigned, with shrieks and shouts and pounding feet, and no one apparently in charge.

The colonel's study door was open, and here Guy found the housekeeper kneeling beside Cressida's unconscious form. There was blood everywhere, and for a moment he forgot to breathe. Then he recovered his composure. 'We have to stop the bleeding. I need a pad of material and strips to bind it to her head.'

Without hesitation, the woman threw back her skirt and ripped what was required from one of her many petticoats. With a folded pad of material in one hand, Guy carefully lifted Cressida's head and clamped it against the gash. 'Quickly — tie the bandages around as tight as you can whilst I keep this in place. My brother did something similar, and this saved his life.'

Once the strips of torn petticoats were in place and the pad of material fixed firmly, he sat back on his heels and took a closer look at the patient. 'Fetch Miss Sarah. Do it now. I need a pillow and rugs to keep Miss Hadley warm. I don't wish to move her until her sister has taken a closer look.'

The housekeeper scrambled up and moments later appeared with the required items. Guy positioned himself behind Cressida, leaning his back against the wall so he could support himself and her quite safely. Then he placed the pillow across his knees and gently placed her head upon it. The willing hands of Miller and a maid wrapped his beloved in the blankets. A red fury consumed him when he saw the unmistakable imprint of a hand on her cheek.

Sarah arrived, closely followed by Amanda and her brother. 'What happened?' she demanded. 'How did Cressie come to be injured?'

'Colonel Hadley struck her.' Guy had to bite back the rest of what he wished to say about that man; he must remember he was the parent of these young people. What he intended to do to the colonel when he found him was best kept to himself.

'I don't understand. Cressie has always been his favourite, and he rarely raised his hand to any of us. Why should he do this to her?' The girl sniffed and stood there wringing her hands when she should have been attending to her sister.

'For God's sake, get down here and take care of Cressida,' Guy said. 'Time enough to discuss what happened when she is out of danger.'

Sarah quickly examined her sister and sat back. 'She's broken no limbs. Her pulse is weak but steady. The bandage you applied appears to be working, but she will need sutures, and I'm not able to do that. We will have to send for a physician.'

A voice Guy didn't immediately recognise spoke from behind his shoulder. 'I can do it. Despite appearances to the contrary, I am a qualified doctor. I completed my training last summer but have yet to set up my shingle.'

Guy twisted and saw it was one of the Forsyth twins speaking. 'Thank God for that. What do you wish me to do? Will you attend to her here, or shall I carry her to her apartment?'

'James Forsyth, in case you're wondering. Let me examine her and then I'll decide. Jack, would you be so kind as to take my medical bag from our chamber to Miss Hadley's apartment?' He knelt beside them and did as Sarah had done before nodding. 'We can move her. She'll be better somewhere warm and comfortable.' As he stood, he briefly squeezed Guy's shoulder. 'Head wounds bleed profusely, my lord, but are rarely as bad as they look. However, the longer she remains insensible, the more worried I shall be.'

Guy shifted back a few inches and then regained his feet. He bent his knees and scooped Cressida up, shocked by the way her arms hung limply at her sides. He carried her through the house and into her bedroom, where the bed was already turned back and two maids were waiting to assist.

'Remove the pillows,' Forsyth instructed. 'I need to have her flat. Place her on her front, Bromley. I shall do the rest.'

Guy did as he was told and then stepped away, not wanting to leave Cressida's side but knowing he was in the way. There were already far too many people crowding into the bed-chamber. 'I think Doctor Forsyth will be better dealing with this matter on his own. Sarah, Amanda, we shall wait next door in her sitting room.' He put an arm around each of them and escorted them out. Sarah was quiet but Amanda was crying quietly. Where were young Hadley and the other Forsyths? Indeed, where was Lady Bromley? Why wasn't she here offering succour and comfort when it was most needed? Guy was determined to find her and get her to explain her garbled remarks.

'I'm going to find my mother. You two remain here until I return.' He was certain they would follow his instructions, as they were too shocked to do anything else. He ran through the house and into the guest wing, and burst into his parent's sitting room without knocking. She was nowhere to be seen, but he could hear voices in her bedchamber. He strode to the door and hammered on it. Not waiting to be invited, he threw open the door and stepped in. His mother was huddled in the arms of her dresser. He was horrified at the change in her appearance. From an attractive middle-aged woman, she'd metamorphosed into an old lady.

Guy was beside her in an instant and gathered her close to his heart. She might be a frivolous woman, but he loved her dearly and couldn't bear to see her so distressed. 'Mama, Cressida is not dead. She has a concussion and an injury to her head, but James Forsyth is a medical man and is taking care of matters as I speak.' He stroked her back and murmured words of encouragement until her crying stopped. Eventually she sniffed and held out a hand for a handkerchief, which her maid stuffed into her outstretched fingers. She blew her nose loudly and then moved away.

'Colonel Hadley asked me to marry him and I agreed. I know it was foolish; we scarcely know each other and are as different as chalk is to cheese. Cressida must have told him he was making a mistake and he reacted violently. I've been sadly mistaken, as he is not the man I thought he was. I could never tie myself to a violent man and wish I'd never agreed to marry him.'

'Mama, I believe you to have been carried away by the unusual circumstances. However, I can assure you it's quite possible to fall in love in the space of a few days. I have asked Cressida to become my wife and she has agreed. I think this was the cause of the disagreement, not anything to do with you and the colonel.'

Immediately her expression changed and her mouth pursed. 'You cannot marry a young lady with no pedigree. I'll not hear of it.'

He stared at her with incomprehension. Did she honestly think he needed her permission to marry? He stood up. 'Cressida and I will be married as soon as it can be arranged. If you do not care to remain at Bromley Court, then I can make arrangements for you to move somewhere else.' He nodded curtly and left her to her sniffles.

How could such a delightful day have turned into a disaster? Guy's desire to exact vengeance on Colonel Hadley had dissipated; there had been more than enough violence in this house already. Hadley and the others must have gone out to find the man. Guy knew he would do better to leave it to them, as whatever his good intentions, if he came face-to-face with the bastard who'd injured his beloved he'd do something he would regret.

18

When Guy returned to Cressida's apartment, Dr Forsyth was talking to the girls. He immediately directed this conversation to the earl. 'I've put in half a dozen sutures and I am satisfied the gash will heal cleanly.' He could not hide his yawn, but instead of apologising he ignored it and continued. 'I found evidence of an earlier injury. Has Miss Hadley taken a tumble in the last two days?'

Guy explained how Cressida had fallen out of the tree. Forsyth's eyes narrowed and he looked less sanguine. 'I'm hoping that Miss Hadley is not unconscious, merely sleeping; but after hearing about her previous accident, I'm not so sure. However, there's nothing anyone can do, so I suggest that we all retire. I shall remain here in case I'm needed.'

'There's no need; I shall be here,' Guy said. 'I must tell you that Cressida is to be my future wife and we intend to be married in the New Year. I believe that was partly the cause of the disagreement between the colonel and herself.'

No one looked particularly surprised at his news. Amanda jumped up and ran across to throw her arms around him. 'We guessed as much, Bromley, and I'm delighted that Cressie will become part of the family.'

Sarah was equally pleased. 'Whatever the parents say about the matter, you will have the support of the rest of us.'

'Thank you for your felicitations. Forsyth is correct — you must return to your beds and try and claim a few hours of sleep before morning. Hopefully the news will be better then.'

Fortunately the girls had not been abed when they were called to the emergency, so had not been obliged to throw on whatever garments they could lay their hands on — unlike Guy, who was standing about in his shirtsleeves. Once everyone had departed, he made his way into the bedchamber to find the maid sitting by her mistress.

'There's no need for you to stay up. I shall take your place.' Her look of absolute horror at his suggestion made him smile. 'Miss Hadley and I are engaged to be married, so it will be quite in order for me to remain here.'

She was on her feet immediately and curtsied deeply. 'In which case, my lord, I shall willingly retire. If you have need of me, just ring the bell.'

He knew the whereabouts of Forsyth, so could send for him if needs be, but he prayed there would be no necessity to call him back tonight. He moved the candelabra closer so he could examine Cressida's face. She was propped on her side in order to prevent the injury from pressing against the pillows. She was unnaturally pale, and when he put his cheek close to her mouth her breathing was barely discernible. He lifted her arm, but it remained limp and flopped back on the covers when he released it. How could Forsyth have gone to his bed when Cressida seemed to be gravely ill? Her skin was clammy and cold.

A hard lump formed in Guy's chest. They had had only Forsyth's word that he was a fully qualified physician. He'd had the correct tools and dealt with the wound efficiently, but did that make him reliable? Guy went to the fire and emptied half the scuttle into it, then threw on half a dozen logs. The room needed to be much warmer and so did Cressida.

Once the fire was roaring, he looked around for further comforters and found a patchwork quilt folded neatly on a shelf in the dressing room. Without giving a moment's heed to protocol or the possible consequences, he climbed onto the bed and tossed the quilt over both of them. Then he removed the pillows that were holding Cressida on her side and placed himself there instead. He slipped his arms around her waist and drew her into his embrace, praying that his body warmth would restore hers.

After half an hour he was convinced her breathing was more regular and her skin much warmer. With a sigh of relief, he relaxed and fell into a deep slumber.

★   ★   ★

He was woken a few hours later by someone shaking his shoulder. 'Bromley, I think it's time you left.'

Blearily he opened one eye to see Dr Forsyth standing beside him, freshly shaved and fully dressed. 'Good God, is it morning already?' His right arm had gone numb from having Cressida's head resting on it all night. He placed his cheek against hers before he rolled away, reassured that her skin was warm and her breathing deep and regular. 'She was too cold and this was the only way I could think to keep her warm. She seems a better colour but has still not woken.'

Forsyth made his own examination and nodded. 'I'm happier with her progress than I was last night, but until she wakes we cannot be sanguine. This is more than sleep. She is comatose, and the longer this continues the less sure I am of a favourable outcome.'

This was not the news that Guy wished to hear. 'I shall get spruced up and return immediately. I don't intend to leave her side until she wakes.' He rubbed his hand across his eyes, hoping the doctor would think it sleep rather than tears he was removing.

His valet had his clothes put out and hot water waiting. He usually shaved himself, but his hands were shaking, so he thought it wiser to allow his man to do it. He was dressed and out of his apartment within a quarter of an hour and back with Cressida.

Forsyth was no longer there, but her maid was tenderly wiping her mistress's face and talking softly to her. Guy retreated without disturbing her; he would wait until she had finished her ministrations. He should have asked Forsyth if the colonel had been located last night.

He checked his watch and saw the time was a little after seven o'clock, but already the house was busy. He headed for the breakfast parlour and found young Hadley and the other three looking pale and drawn. 'You didn't find Colonel Hadley?' he asked them.

'No. We spent an hour searching and then were forced to return because of the cold.' Hadley was unshaven and looked as if he'd slept in his clothes. 'I don't condone his behaviour, but I'd not wish him to die because of it, and I fear it might have come to that. Jack reckons he wouldn't have survived outside last night, especially as he rushed off in his evening clothes without the benefit of outdoor garments or boots.' He blinked away tears before continuing. 'Thank God my sister is no worse.'

Guy helped himself to coffee, but had little appetite so ignored the buffet. He was about to respond when his brother appeared, using his crutches for the first time. He was the only one amongst them who looked well rested.

'Good morning, Harry. You seem adept with those. Take a seat and I'll bring you your breakfast.' Guy waited until everyone was settled before speaking. 'I'm not sure how much any of you know about last night, but things have changed, and you ought to know about it. Colonel Hadley asked my mother to marry him and she accepted — although she has changed her mind after what happened. Cressida and I are betrothed and shall be married with or without our parents' approval as soon as can be arranged.'

Richard seemed unsurprised by the news. 'In which case, Bromley, you'd better pray that my father is still alive — because if he isn't, the family will be in mourning for months, and there will be no weddings.'

Jack Forsyth slapped his friend on the back, forcing him to spray his coffee on the tablecloth. 'Look on the bright side, old fellow. At least you won't be sent to darkest India, and will inherit this place and be a very wealthy man.'

Guy's fingers closed around his cup and his eyes narrowed. 'That was a damned stupid thing to say. I suggest you remove yourself before I throw you out head first.'

The young man he'd addressed scrambled to his feet and was backing nervously towards the door. Guy put down his cup with slow deliberation, and this was enough to send Forsyth out of the breakfast parlour. In the silence that followed his departure, his running footsteps were clearly audible. Would his brothers now object?

Richard stared at Guy as if he were seeing him for the first time. 'That was impressive, my lord. I've never seen Jack move so fast. Thank you for your intervention, but it was unnecessary. He's famous for making jests in poor taste.'

Guy sipped his coffee thoughtfully

before answering. 'In which case, it's high time he stopped. The last few hours have been a catalogue of disasters, and I sincerely hope that there will be a positive outcome for your father. I know that your sister will make a full recovery.'

'I sent out a dozen men to search for my father before I came to break my fast. I intend to change my clothes and then join them.'

'You will understand if I don't offer to assist you,' Guy said, and the young man nodded.

Grimshaw appeared at the door and cleared his throat noisily. When he had their attention, he made his announcement. 'The master spent the night in the stables and is now safely in his apartment.'

A collective sigh of relief rippled around the table until it reached Guy, who felt a wave of rage engulf him. This was another black mark against the man for allowing three young men to risk their lives looking for him when he was snug in the stables. He lowered his eyes and fought to control his temper. He was a guest in this house and intended to become a member of the family; and however much he wished to break every bone in the colonel's body, the man was soon to become his father-in-law.

Harry poured himself a second cup of coffee and said casually, 'This is going to be a most unusual Christmas with you wanting to murder our host, Mama not speaking to either of you, and Cressida too unwell to join us. Not forgetting the fact that Jack will be too terrified to speak to you in future.' He took a noisy swig of his drink and then continued. 'The pantomime must be cancelled, as well as all the other activities Mama had planned, which will thoroughly upset the staff and make them surly.'

This pronouncement was made in such a sombre tone that Guy's anger dissipated, and reluctantly he smiled. He raised his cup in salute to his brother's clever ploy to defuse the situation. 'You paint a fascinating picture of the days to come, Harry. Perhaps it would be wiser for all of us to remain in our apartments until the snow thaws and we can depart.' This suggestion was taken in the spirit in which it was made. Harry laughed, Richard protested, and the remaining Forsyth brothers summoned up a smile from somewhere. 'I'm returning to Cressida's apartment. No doubt the girls will be down soon, and you can tell them how things are progressing.'

Guy considered visiting his mother but thought better of it. He was in no mood for her silliness, and it would be better for both of them if they remained separate, at least until Cressida was out of danger and he was in a more equitable frame of mind.

* * *

Cressida was roused from her stupor by an urgent need for the commode. She attempted to sit up, but her head spun unpleasantly and she feared she was about to cast up her accounts.

'Let me help you, sweetheart,' Guy said beside her. 'You sustained a nasty injury last night and have been unconscious ever since.'

The very last person she wished to help her to relieve herself was her future husband. 'Go away, Guy. I need my maid most urgently.'

He understood immediately, but instead of vanishing as instructed he scooped her out of bed and carried her into the dressing room, where the required receptacle was kept during the day. Polly was at Cressida's side and supported her so Guy could make a tactful exit.

When Cressida was done, her maid helped her to her feet, but they both realised they would need assistance to get her back to bed. Guy must have heard her moving as he tapped on the door, and when given leave to enter he picked her up a second time and strode back to place her gently in her bed again.

'How are you feeling?' he asked. 'I can't tell you how relieved I am that you're awake at last.'

'I've a frightful headache, feel dizzy, and my stomach is horribly unsettled, but apart from that I'm perfectly well.' The side of her face was painful and she raised a hand to touch her cheek, only then remembering how she'd come to be hurt. Her eyes brimmed over and she tried to gulp back a sob.

'Don't cry, my love. All will be well. I haven't killed your father, in case you were concerned, although I should dearly like to take a horsewhip to him.'

The ice in Guy's voice sent a chill down Cressida's spine, and her tears dried. She explained to him what had taken place, and he was unsurprised by her revelations. 'Mama didn't hold with physical punishment, and my father was rarely here when we were growing up. I recall that he thrashed Richard once or twice, but he never raised a hand to

Sarah or me. He has always had a shocking temper, but I'd no idea he could be violent.'

'I've yet to see him, as he's hiding in his rooms. But you can be very sure when I do speak to him, he'll not enjoy the experience.'

'Are our families to be doubly related, or will this incident put paid to the romance between our parents?'

'My mother has changed her mind, but it's quite possible she will change it back again as she's as contrary as a weathervane. However, this situation can be turned to our advantage. Your father can hardly refuse permission for our nuptials after this. I must tell you that Mama has objected strenuously to our engagement, but I've told her it's none of her business. As soon as the weather allows and you are well again, we shall depart. Now that Harry can move about on crutches, he is quite capable of making the journey.'

When Guy told her what had taken place in the breakfast parlour, Cressida smiled. 'Harry's quite correct; the next few days are going to be decidedly strange. I see no reason why the pantomime should not go ahead even if I am unable to participate myself. Sarah or Amanda can read my part — after all, neither of our parents has bothered to learn their lines.'

Guy had carried over a chair and was sitting close beside her, but the height of her bed meant she had to look down at him, which was a novel situation for both of them. After a few minutes he said something extremely rude under his breath and kicked the chair away. 'Do you mind if I join you on your bed with my boots on? I'm quite prepared to remove them if you do.'

'I rather think the question is, do I mind you joining me on the bed at all.'

He smiled his heart-stopping smile. For a second she couldn't think straight, and it was nothing to do with her head injury. 'Well, darling girl,' he said, 'do I have your permission?'

'If you put a cloth underneath your

feet, then I'm sure Polly will not object.'

The bed was more than big enough to accommodate several people, and he could've positioned himself in such a way that there was a large gap between them. However, he plumped up the pillows and settled himself so close that when she inhaled she could smell the lemon verbena he'd used at his morning ablutions.

His arm insinuated itself around her shoulders and she relaxed into his embrace. For a while she could forget the difficulties she would face when she emerged from her bedchamber. The fire was crackling in the grate, and Guy's breathing was deep and even beside her, so she closed her eyes and drifted off to sleep in the arms of the man she loved.

19

When Cressida woke, there were candles lit and Guy had gone. The bed felt empty without him, which was quite extraordinary. How could she feel so comfortable in his company in such an intimate setting, when she'd known him for only a few days?

Although her head ached, she was no longer dizzy; but was ravenous and her stomach gurgled loudly. Polly called out cheerfully from the dressing room, 'I'm just going down to fetch your supper tray, miss. I've been waiting for you to wake. Do you wish me to help you to the commode first?'

'No, thank you. I need to eat before I do anything else. Make sure Cook doesn't send up broth, but something more substantial and tasty.' She smiled at this shouted exchange. Even her abigail was behaving strangely, for a week ago she wouldn't have dreamt of yelling, and certainly not about such a delicate matter.

Talking was painful, as not only did it pull on the stitches in the back of her head, but also hurt the side of her face where her father had struck her. How could he have done such a thing to a daughter he professed to love? Was it his association with Lady Bromley that had changed his character so quickly, and not for the better? This lady had now become a stranger to her and was no longer Aunt Elizabeth in her head, and would certainly not be referred to so informally in future. It was a mystery to her how Guy's mother could believe it perfectly acceptable for a dowager countess to marry a colonel, but not for an earl to marry the colonel's daughter.

Cressida decided to make her way into her sitting room and eat her supper at the table, as she disliked eating from a tray across her lap. By moving slowly and not turning her head too swiftly, she was able to gain her feet. Her bedrobe was conveniently draped over the end of the bed, and she managed to negotiate the difficult task of putting her arms through the sleeves and then tying the belt around her waist.

After a cautious step away from her bed, she remained stationary, waiting to see if her legs gave way beneath her or her head spun unpleasantly as it had done before. But no; apart from feeling a trifle weak, she was perfectly capable of making her way, albeit slowly, to the more convivial surroundings of her sitting room.

As it got dark so early nowadays, that was no indication as to the actual time, and she'd neglected to look at the mantel clock before setting off. Presumably Guy had departed to change for dinner, but she was confident he would return to see her afterwards.

How were things progressing downstairs? Would Lady Bromley and the colonel come out of hiding or remain closeted in their apartments? Cressida was relieved when she reached the safety of her chaise longue and was able to settle comfortably. Polly would have to move a suitable table when she returned with the tray.

The clock above the fire stated that the time was a little after four o'clock — small wonder she was starving.

★ ★ ★

Guy was tempted to send his apologies downstairs and have a tray sent to Cressida's apartment so they could eat together. However, he was determined to speak to the colonel, and could not do so if he didn't go down for dinner.

There'd been no communication from his mother, and he had decided that the first move to reconciliation must come from her. He glanced at his watch — four o'clock. He would find Colonel Hadley and speak his piece before the others came down.

On enquiry, he discovered his quarry was in his study, and headed that way. He rapped on the door but didn't wait to be asked to enter. He stepped in ready to verbally tear the man apart, but what he saw before him changed his mind.

The man slumped over an empty decanter bore no resemblance to the upright, handsome gentleman he'd met just four days ago. This person had somehow deteriorated into an old man — and a very drunk old man at that. The colonel gazed at him with blurry eyes as if not recognising him. Then, as Guy stood immobile in the doorway, recognition dawned. He had thought it impossible for the colonel to look any more wretched, but somehow he managed it. The man had been punished enough, and as his future son-in-law it behoved him to do what he could to restore the colonel's dignity.

Guy closed the door behind him and walked in with what he hoped was a non-threatening manner towards the desk. He put his hands on it and leaned forward. 'Colonel Hadley, what you did was reprehensible, but your daughter and I are prepared to put the matter behind us.'

He wasn't sure that Cressida would be able to do this, but he was certain she wouldn't want to see her father in such a poor case. His words got no reaction so he tried again. 'Cressida is almost fully recovered, and will be able to come down tomorrow to celebrate our Lord's birthday. You must pull yourself together and sober up. There's still time to save this Christmas house party from total disaster.'

Finally the colonel reacted. He put down his glass and pushed himself straight with some difficulty. 'My temper could have killed the person I love most in this world. How can she forgive me when I can't forgive myself?'

Guy looked around for a chair and selected a plain wooden one and fetched it. He spun it and straddled the seat, then rested his forearms on the back. 'A good start, sir, would be to announce our engagement tonight and give us your blessing. I think you had best forget the arrangement you made with my mother; she's against my marriage and has changed her mind about her own.'

'I'll do that and willingly, my lord. My daughter won't wish to reside under the roof of the man who struck her down so cruelly. And another thing — I've decided I can hardly send my son away for what he did when I've behaved so badly myself.' He attempted to push himself upright and failed. 'I fear I'm a trifle bosky, my lord. I need to return to my apartment and get ready for dinner.'

Immediately Guy was beside him and assisted him to his feet. Then, with his arm around the colonel's waist, he guided him to the door. It took the assistance of two footmen to get the inebriated gentleman up the stairs, and Guy left them to it and headed for his brother's chambers. The sitting-room door was open and he could hear more than one voice talking inside. It sounded as if the remaining gentlemen were gathered together and that this was more an altercation than a conversation. Damn it to hell! What next?

He strode in and stared at the assembled company. Young Hadley halted in mid-sentence and gaped at him. Silence followed before those who were capable stood and bowed, and even Harry looked alarmed.

'What the devil is going on in here? Do I need to knock some heads together?'

One of the Forsyth brothers was sidling behind the other two, and the doctor was left to speak for the three of them. Harry had nothing to say and neither did Hadley.

'I beg your pardon, my lord,' Forsyth began. 'We've been imbibing vast quantities of brandy all afternoon, and I doubt that any of us can recall how the argument started.' He was obliged to enunciate each syllable carefully in order not to slur his words.

'Good God, that's all I need. Hadley,

I found your father drunk as a wheelbarrow in his study and decidedly the worse for wear. The good news is that he has given his blessing to my engagement and has decided not to send you off to India after all. I've sent him upstairs with a tray of strong coffee in the hope he will be sober enough to join us for dinner.'

'What about Mama?' Harry asked. 'I take it she's still *persona non grata* with you? She came to visit me and told me she'd changed her mind about marrying the colonel. Can't say I blame her after what happened — however, her disapproval of Cressie is unacceptable; and until she apologises and welcomes your future wife into the family, she'd do best to remain in seclusion.'

Harry was obviously not drunk. 'Exactly,' Guy agreed. 'Gentlemen, you have less than an hour to sort yourselves out and appear suitably contrite and properly dressed for dinner. I suggest that you return to your rooms immediately.'

He didn't need to make the suggestion a second time as the room emptied in seconds, leaving him alone with his brother. 'Well done, Bromley,' Harry said. 'You've got the measure of those four. They were squabbling over the last game of billiards — a large sum of money was wagered and they couldn't agree on the score or who was the winner. Even Jonathan became involved, which is unlike him.'

'I suppose I'd better go and see our parent and try and persuade her to change her mind. Not about marrying Colonel Hadley — I can't see that being a successful union; but she has to accept Cressida as my future wife or she will find herself living in Northumbria.'

'Dinner should be interesting this evening, Bromley. You've put the fear of God into my friends, and they will be gibbering idiots by the end of the evening if you don't stop glaring at them.'

Guy picked up a nearby cushion and

tossed it at his brother. 'Having a broken leg doesn't seem to have suppressed your high spirits, Harry, and I thank God for it. Whatever transpires this evening, can I rely on you to help defuse any unpleasantness?'

His brother waved the cushion in the air. 'You can always count on me. We Bromley brothers stick together.'

There was ample time to speak to Lady Bromley before they had to come down, but there was a danger she would be in the middle of her preparations and unwilling to see her son. Guy knew he must risk that, because he wanted to have matters straight between them before they met in public.

He knocked on her sitting-room door and walked straight in, surprised to see his parent in a day gown and looking as if she intended to remain that way. 'You will be pleased to know, madam, that my future wife is out of danger and should be back downstairs tomorrow. As you're not in your boudoir changing, I'm assuming you don't intend to come down tonight.'

'I'm pleased to hear that Miss Hadley is recovering. And you are right in your assumption; I shall not come down again until we are able to leave this place.'

'You cannot sulk in here for another two weeks, Mama. Not only would it be the height of incivility, but it would also be ridiculous.'

She tossed her head like a girl half her age. 'Coming down would mean being obliged to speak to Colonel Hadley, and that would be embarrassing after I have jilted him. Also, my opinion of your intended nuptials stands, and mixing with this family will make it seem as if I approve of your inappropriate liaison.'

Guy turned away and took several deep breaths before he had his fury under control. He had no wish to exacerbate the matter by saying something he might later regret. After all, however much he disliked her opinion, his mother still deserved a modicum of respect.

'Madam, you give me no option. Unless you accept my choice of bride and welcome her into the family, you will not return to Bromley Court, but must remove yourself at once to Blanton Manor in Northumbria. Amanda will remain with me, and my wife will oversee her debut and see that she finds herself a suitable husband.'

He turned away but didn't make a hasty exit, hoping that his decision would prompt his mother to change her mind. But she said nothing, and he left her apartment wishing things could be different. He loved her despite her faults, but his beloved Cressida must now come first, and he wouldn't tolerate her being treated as if she were his inferior.

He headed for his fiancée's chambers, knowing that spending time with her would restore his happiness. Instead of remaining on the first floor, he decided to detour and check that everything was running smoothly, as there had been no one in charge of the household today.

The festive atmosphere of the central hall lifted his spirits. The best beeswax candles had been used in the garlands and these had been lit. He could hardly credit it was Christmas Eve, he was about to banish his mother to the wilds of the north, his brother had a broken leg, and he himself had fallen in love for the first time in his life.

He wandered from room to room, admiring the decorations and enjoying the atmosphere, and even went into the ballroom, which still had the scenery for the abandoned pantomime set up on the dais at the far end. He closed his eyes and sent a fervent prayer up to the Almighty in the hope that He might be listening, and asked that his mother would give up her intransigence and they could celebrate Christmas Day together as they had always done in the past.

Cressida had finished her meal and the debris had been removed when Guy strolled in. His smile was brilliant, but she detected sadness in his eyes. She patted the empty space beside her and he sat down. 'What is troubling you, my love? Did you not manage to settle things with our parents?'

'I told your father you had forgiven him. If you'd seen how wretched he was, you might have done so yourself. He has given his permission for our union and will announce it at dinner tonight. However, my mother remains determined to be disagreeable, and she will be moving to Northumbria as soon as we return home.'

Cressida was horrified at his announcement. 'You cannot do that! It would be too cruel. Is there not somewhere nearby she could move to until she becomes used to the idea? I promise you that when the first grandchild arrives, she will change her tune.'

Guy reached out and lifted her onto his lap and she didn't object, although she knew this would be considered inappropriate if anyone was to hear of it. 'How is your head, darling? You have a shocking bruise on your face, your hair is tangled, and that bandage is hardly flattering — but you are still the most beautiful woman in the world to me.'

'Thank you, I think. I was hoping to come down for church tomorrow, but if my injuries are so obvious, it would be better to remain here until the bruise has faded. I've no wish to become the subject of unpleasant speculation from the congregation.'

'I doubt that you will be feeling well enough to walk half a mile in the snow. Better stay here in the warm with Harry. The house looks beautiful, and I shall insist that we do the same at Bromley Court in future.'

He had deliberately avoided answering her request not to banish Lady Bromley, but if he had forgiven her father for his violence, he must do the same for his mother. Cressida was determined to persuade him to change his mind. Christmas was a time for celebration, for goodwill to all men, and these family rifts must be mended.

'I wish you to carry me downstairs after dinner,' Cressida said. 'I'll change into something a little smarter. I want to make sure my father knows I forgive him, and I want you to do the same for your mother. Is that agreed?'

'Are you saying you can accept my mother's rejection?'

'As I said before, she will soon change her tune when we have children for her to fuss over.' The thought of what they must do first in order to produce these progeny sent waves of heat chasing around her body.

Guy tilted her back so he could cover her mouth with his. This kiss was gentle and her lips softened, but when his hot tongue slid between her teeth everything changed. She no longer knew, nor cared, what liberties he took; all she wanted was to continue this passionate exchange until its conclusion.

Suddenly she was tipped from his lap and he was standing with his back to her by the door. Had she offended him with her wanton behaviour? When he spoke his voice was gruff, almost unrecognisable.

'I want to make love to you, sweetheart, but we must not pre-empt our wedding night. I shall leave you now and come back for you after we've eaten. I promise you that everything will be as it should be. I shall speak to my mother immediately and tell her that I accept her reservations, but as long as she is civil to you I don't require her to congratulate us.'

'As long as she is prepared to attend our wedding, I don't care if she remains aloof. Please tell her that you'll not send her away. I couldn't bear that.'

He turned, but didn't come any closer. 'I love you, Cressida. You make me the happiest of men.'

'How soon do you intend for us to be

married? Could you obtain a special licence?' Her heart was trying to escape from her bodice, and a strange restlessness made her shift uncomfortably.

His eyes blazed. 'I'll send one of the grooms by post to London. He'll not be able to go until Boxing Day, but he should be able to obtain what we want and be back here before Twelfth Night. Are you sure you want to be married as soon as that?'

She nodded, her mouth too dry to say what she really wanted. His eyes glittered in the candlelight. 'I'll see you in a couple of hours.'

They were the longest two hours of Cressida's life and also the most significant. She changed and dismissed Polly, telling her that she had no need of her services until the morning.

When Guy appeared, she was waiting for him, not in her sitting room but in her prettiest nightgown in her bedroom. If they were to be married in less than a sennight, it hardly mattered if they pre-empted their wedding night.

'Are you sure, my darling?'

She nodded. 'I love you, and cannot wait another minute to share everything I have with you.'

Guy needed no further reassurances. He kicked the door shut behind him and was at her side in two strides.

CHRISTMAS AT CASTLE ELRICK

Fenella J. Miller

Severely injured in the Napoleonic Wars, Sir Ralph Elrick has been brooding in his castle for years, waiting for Miss Verity Sanderson to reach her majority and marry him. The week before Christmas, she sets off to his ancestral home to become his wife. But Castle Elrick is a cold, unwelcoming place — and Ralph and his small staff are not the only residents. Will Christmas be a joyous celebration, or will the ghosts of Castle Elrick force the newlyweds apart?